THE WITCH WHO HATED HALLOWEEN

FELIX AND PENZI'S SEVENTH PARANORMAL MYSTERY

KATIE PENRYN

Cover based on a design by
BOOKCOVERARTISTRY.COM

Published by
KARIBU PUBLISHERS SAS

THE WITCH WHO HATED HALLOWEEN

**Penzi's always hated Halloween.
This year it's the pits, the worst one ever.
Her supernatural arch enemy is out to get her.**

While Penzi is busy cleaning up the mess left in the town cemetery by local vandals, her foe launches his attack. Once Penzi becomes aware of his assault, she knows she's tempting fate by carrying on with the work. However, *La Toussaint* (All Saint's Day) is one of the most important festivals of the year in France.

The townspeople of Beaucoup-sur-Mer can't be allowed to find their holy site in such a state of desecration. Penzi and Felix must see the job through to the end and ready the vaults and graves for the next day's family visits despite the mounting danger.

This time it's a fight to the death between Penzi and her arch enemy.

Will her bodyguard, the shape shifting leopard Felix, be there to lend tooth and claw as the natural and supernatural worlds collide on this most spooky night of the year?

ALSO BY KATIE PENRYN

Available from your favorite bookseller.
Links on katiepenryn.com

French Country Murders

1 - The Witch who Couldn't Spell
2 - The Witch who Loved Éclairs
3 - The Witch who Got the Blues
4 - The Witch who Found a Pearl
5 - The Witch who Saved Christmas
6 - The Witch who Foiled the Plot
7 - The Witch who Hated Halloween
8 - The Witch who Risked the Shot
9 - The Witch who Picked a Poppy
In development:
10 - The Witch who Forged a Monet
11 - The Witch who Tipped the Scales

This series is also available in Large Print and Ebook.

Our Man in Mazita

1 - Beau--ootiful Soo--oop!
2 - Something Spotted
3 - Something Rotten
4 - Christmas in Mazita

~

**The WITCH who
HATED HALLOWEEN**

French Country Murders
Book 7

Copyright © 2017 by Katie Penryn
KatiePenryn.com

Cover based on a design by
BookCoverArtistry.com

Published by
Karibu Publishers SAS

CONTENTS

You will find Chapter 1 of the next book in the French Country Murders mysteries series, **_The Witch who Risked the Shot_**, on Page 89.

There is a **_Glossary_** of French words and expressions used in this series on Page 101.

1

———

(*La Toussaint* is the French for All Saints' Day and is pronounced *La-too-san(d)*, like *sand* without the *d*.)

"Vandals. Grave robbers. Here in Beaucoup-sur-Mer. What is the world coming to?" asked the mayor, Monsieur Bonhomie, as he heaved himself out of his executive chair, or tried to.

He wasn't getting any slimmer. Too many of those delicious little sponge *madeleines* he always offered us when we visited his office at the *mairie*.

Stuck at that awkward angle that makes your thighs ache, jammed half in half out by the arms of the chair, he let out a wail, "Help me, Penzi."

I threw my purse down on a chair and rushed around the desk to aid the poor man. Felix, my shape shifting bodyguard, beat me to it on his other side.

"Push his honor back down, or pull him out?" Felix asked me as he tried to suppress a grin.

"Heave," I said suiting action to word and taking hold of one of the mayor's arms and bracing a foot against the chair's metal pedestal.

Felix grabbed the other and none too gently we tore the mayor from his seat. We turned away to give him a few moments to restore his dignity: tuck in his shirt and pull down his waistcoat. When we turned back, he was wiping his perspiring forehead with his giant handkerchief.

He tossed a rueful grin our way. "That chair gets smaller by the day."

"If you say so, monsieur," said Felix. He rolled the offending seat away against the wall and replaced it with an armless chair. "Try this one for size until you can buy something bigger."

Monsieur Bonhomie gingerly lowered his massive buttocks.

"It really isn't my day," he said as he scooted the chair forward to squeeze his thighs under his desk. "It started badly with a call from Father Pedro. That's why I phoned you. I hope I haven't put you out, Penzi, calling at such short notice?"

"Not at all. Felix and I were ready to leave the house anyway for a trip to the shopping mall to find a Halloween costume for my young brother, Jimbo."

The mayor made a French moue and a half shrug. "Don't talk to me about Halloween. I hate it. Silly American commercialism polluting our culture from across the Atlantic."

"I wouldn't put it that strongly," I replied, "but have to admit I don't like Halloween either. In fact, I hate it."

Felix raised his eyebrows at me. This was our second Halloween together, and I hadn't said anything against the festival the year before. However, I was saved from answering either the mayor or Felix by the secretary who came in with the now customary tray of English tea and French *madeleines*, the latter being the poor mayor's undoing.

Felix took the tray from the secretary and laid it on the desk. "Why did you want to see us, monsieur?" he asked.

I poured out. "And what's all this about vandals? You seem very angry," I said as I passed the mayor his tea.

"Place it on the desk for me, Penzi. I'm spitting mad. I don't trust myself not to spill it."

Felix and I drank our tea and ate a couple of the sponge cakes while the mayor took deep breaths until his color had receded and his hands had stopped shaking.

"Well, monsieur?" I prompted him.

He inhaled once more right down to the pit of his lungs and let the breath out slowly. "Here we are doing our best to get Beaucoup-sur-Mer back on the average tourist's itinerary, and our own people are sabotaging our efforts."

"In what way?"

The mayor gave a big harrumph. "Our very own people stabbing us in the back. How's it going to look when this gets out?"

"Monsieur, it would help if you told us what's happened. It's not another murder, is it?" I asked, hoping against hope that we weren't in for another spate of killings in our quiet little seaside town.

"It's murder, yes, but not of a person. Our culture and our religious sensibilities are being attacked. Father Pedro says someone has been covering the vaults and the cemetery walls with hideous graffiti."

My spirits rose. That I could deal with. A good

scrubbing brush and bucket of hot water or paint stripper, as the case may be, and all would be pristine again. Who would do the work I didn't know. If we could catch the culprits, I'd make sure they did.

"That's not too bad," I said. "We can get that sorted out pronto."

"How quick is pronto?" the mayor asked leaning forward and glaring at me.

I shrank back astonished at his aggression. What was wrong with the man?

"I see you don't understand the urgency, Penzi. It's not your fault. You are not a Catholic, and you are not French."

"Guilty on both counts," I answered sitting back and making a conscious effort not to be offended. The mayor was to be respected. He must have his reasons for being so distressed and, quite honestly, rather rude.

Felix on the other hand bridled at the mayor's remarks. "Monsieur, Penzi is your friend. She's helped you out many times. She's enthusiastic about your public relations scheme to recapture the town's good reputation. You can't fault her for that."

The mayor raised his eyes up to heaven with a heavy sigh. "I'm not being offensive, well, I don't mean to be. I'm simply stating the facts. As an English non-Catholic, Penzi is probably not aware of the significance of this week. It's Saturday already. On Tuesday it will be the 31st October with this new fangled Halloween business—"

"With respect, monsieur," I said, "although I don't personally like Halloween, it isn't a *new* festival. As you must know, it's based on the old Celtic festival of Samhain, the celebration of the end of the harvest season and the beginning of the long days of winter."

"All this dressing up as ghosts and witches... and the

fuss about pumpkins. That's new. And the corporations are making so much money out of it. Anyway, as I was saying, Tuesday is this Halloween, but for us it's November 1st which is the important day. That's *La Toussaint*. Even though we're a secular country with complete separation of church and state, and in spite of everything the French Revolution tried to do to kill religion, we are at rock bottom a Christian society for the most part."

"I'm aware of that, monsieur," I said anxious to soothe his ruffled feathers. "Halloween to us in England is All Hallows' Eve and *La Toussaint* is our All Saints' Day."

"But for us French, *La Toussaint* is one of the most important festivals of the year. Even people who are not religious for most of the year, observe *La Toussaint*. It's a public holiday here. All the Christian citizens of Beaucoup-sur-Mer will visit the cemetery on the day to place flowers on the graves of their ancestors and show their respect. What are they going to say when they see the tombs and vaults covered in graffiti?"

"You mentioned the walls as well."

"Yes, that, too. It's all such a nightmare and so complicated. Although the head of each family has to take care of their family's tombs, as mayor I'm the one responsible for the maintenance of the cemetery. In the circumstances, I can't expect the townspeople to deal with this vandalism. This will touch at the heart of the commune. I'll be lucky to be elected again if this gets out."

"So, you'd like us to help you, monsieur?" I asked.

"Oh Penzi, I'll be grateful for ever. If you could find the culprits. Work with Inspector Dubois on this. It is criminal damage after all. And perhaps Felix could organize a working party to clean up the paint."

"Shouldn't the vandals be made to do that?" I asked.

The mayor gave me a look of exasperation. "In an ideal world, but time is pressing. People will be visiting the cemetery between now and Wednesday to tidy up their family graves and tombs before *La Toussaint*. I don't want them seeing the damage."

"Right," I said rising to my feet. "The sooner we get going the better."

Felix paused before joining me at the door. He asked the mayor for a letter of authority to handle the clean-up. Monsieur Bonhomie undertook to email one to us *tout de suite,* in other words ASAP.

"WHAT DO you make of that, boss?" Felix asked as he took my elbow to help me down the steps out of the *mairie*.

"At least it's not a murder. Let's be thankful for that. I can turn it to good advantage by writing an article about the difference between Halloween in France, England and the States. Have you brought your camera along?"

"It's in the car. And yours?"

"Always."

We decided to take a ten-minute break down at the Esplanade, so we could plan our campaign and make the necessary phone calls. Autumn in the South West of France was the best time of the year for me. The summer was way too hot and the winters were long and wet. The day was glorious, bright sunbeams glancing off the waves lapping the perfect crescent of the beach down below the Esplanade. Away out to sea the fishing fleet chugged past on its way home to the port of Darennes.

In the glow of the Indian summer, I threw off my fleece and ordered an iced coffee, hoping it wasn't the last one of the season. Felix stayed faithful to tea, livening it up with a dash of Laphroaig from his companion silver hip-flask.

"Phone calls first, Felix. See if you can get Inspector Dubois to meet us in about half an hour at the cemetery. If so, give Father Pedro a ring and ask him to meet us there with the town's head *cantonnier*."

I should explain that the *cantonnier* is the gardener employed by the commune via the mayor's office to maintain the public spaces which, according to what the mayor had said, included the cemetery but excluded the tombs and graves themselves.

While I sipped my delicious iced coffee through a paper straw, ever mindful of plastic pollution, Felix contacted Inspector Dubois and Father Pedro. Inspector Dubois was the head of the local *gendarmerie*. As such he wouldn't normally be called in to handle a small matter like vandalism, but the mayor knew we had a reasonably good working relationship. For my part, I knew Dubois fancied me and so was usually ready to be helpful even if he did stay competitive. Father Pedro we'd met several times. A kind man who'd helped Felix and our female dog Zig with their fear of bees. He was our local parish priest, Roman Catholic, of course, and from Spain because the number of French priests had fallen fifty per cent in the past twenty years and two-thirds of those remaining were over sixty-five.

Felix swiped off his phone and called the waiter over for another cup of tea.

"I've set up a meeting for quarter past twelve. Father Pedro has a catechism class this morning. Dubois is on duty but can't get away until lunchtime. The gardener, a Pierre Lamy, is working at the cemetery today, anyway, clearing the paths ready for *La Toussaint*. It was he who phoned Father Pedro about the damage."

"Good. That gives us time to call in at the shopping mall on the way."

I drained my coffee and waited impatiently for Felix to drink down his tea. Fortunately, a cup of tea in France is usually served tepid. The French do not understand tea. Coffee, yes, but tea, no.

2

———

When I received the call from the mayor that morning I'd changed my plans about taking Jimbo shopping to find him a Halloween costume and had left him at home with Gwinny, our mother. Fortunately, I had thought to check his measurements. I pulled into the parking area of the local shopping mall and clambered out ready to search out a killer disguise for Jimbo despite my personal feelings about Halloween.

Felix must have read my thoughts because as we strolled arm-in-arm across to the entrance, he asked me why I hated Halloween.

"You'll think me a scaredy cat," I began.

"Never," he interrupted me. "You're one of the bravest people I know. Remember, how I was frightened of bees. That was pretty stupid."

"Well, thank you for that," I answered giving him a quick squeeze on his forearm. "I hated Halloween as a child. All those horrible ghosts and skeletons. And I didn't like trick or treating; knocking on strangers' doors in the dark. Gwinny still lived with us in those days. She didn't like Halloween either and her attitude may have rubbed off on me. She had to come with us to keep us safe."

"Did you ever ask her why she didn't like Halloween?"

"No. I didn't get a chance. By the time I thought of doing so, she'd run off for her seven-year sabbatical from motherhood."

Felix pushed the door open for me and we entered the mall to be met by the overpowering smell of chrysanthemums. I'd forgotten about that. Only a narrow pathway had been left for customers around the sides of the foyer. In the middle was a vast carpet of yellow and bronze potted plants. I'd seen this for the first time the previous year and had been stunned. So many chrysanthemums all laid out at once. In England, that would be a florist's dream. There they are a highly prized cut flower in the autumn... and expensive to boot.

"Wow!" said Felix. "Not something I ever saw in the Middle Congo."

"Nor in England," I added. "Last year, I asked Audrey about them."

Audrey was a friend of ours who lived above a shop she rented called *The Union Jack*, which was to be found facing the bottom of our street and which stocked all the little titbits and delicacies a Brit cannot live without.

"She told me," I went on, "that some people call the chrysanthemum *the flower of death* because of its association with All Saints' Day. She warned me never to give them as a present as the gift could be thought offensive or, even worse, a harbinger of the Grim Reaper."

Felix gave me a nudge. "Come along, boss. Stop being so maudlin. If you think about it, it's a practical flower for this time of year. It blooms in autumn when little else does. That must have been how the custom started in the days before air delivery of flowers all around the world at any time of the year. The people here need flowers to put on the graves on *La Toussaint* and a potted 'mum does the trick and probably lasts until the frost."

I shrugged off the feeling of doom aroused in me by the sight of so many soon-to-be grave adornments. Maybe I was looking at things the wrong way. They weren't a token of death as such, they were a symbol of the respect the people would pay to their ancestors and that's what I should concentrate on – respect not death.

We carried on to the end of the mall where it opened out into a hypermarket. I'd seen in the publicity pamphlets our postwoman, Martine Courrier, had delivered that this shop had a large display of children's Halloween costumes. To reach it, we walked past a five-yard long display of artificial flowers in pots, bought in especially for *La Toussaint*.

Felix looked at me sideways. "Must be an awful lot of dead people round here."

I gave him a shove. "Felix, don't you dare say something like that. Someone will hear you and be offended. Remember you are a guest in this country. One with dodgy papers."

But he had brought a smile to my face. However, as I'd feared, the photos of the costumes had made them look a hundred times better than they were in real life.

"I must make Jimbo's costume next year. These are tawdry. Chinese rubbish," I said, swishing the hangers backwards and forwards in an effort to find something interesting.

"Did he say what he wanted?" asked Felix.

"A pirate or a leopard."

"They don't have either of those. This is Halloween not

a fancy dress party. How about a vampire, with fake blood and long pointed teeth?"

"It'll have to do. We'll be late for our meeting if we take any longer."

So we bought the vampire costume and hoped Jimbo would at least be happy with it if not ecstatic.

WE FOUND PIERRE LAMY, the gardener, hard at work weeding between the monuments to the afterlife. He was a tall wiry man in his middle thirties with a pencil thin mustache, his dark hair cut short with a fashionable quiff at the front. We exchanged civilities and asked him to show us the damage, not that we needed him to. It was only too apparent.

The semi-literate French equivalent of English four-letter words stood out in garish colors of neon orange, ultramarine and scarlet all around the inner perimeter of the graveyard, a space half the size of a football pitch. Not a vault nor a tomb nor a simple grave had been spared as far as the eye could see. These spray painted scribblings were not the work of a Banksy or a So What Parisian artist. They were mere desecrations of a holy place.

I turned to Lamy. "This is a stupendous task. It'll take a team of a dozen men a week to undo this abhorrence."

"And we simply don't have the time," he said, his brows knitting together with anxiety at the thought of what the citizens of Beaucoup-sur-Mer would think of him and his gang of gardeners.

"Let's take a proper look," suggested Felix, "before we give in to despair."

Leaving Lamy behind, Felix took my hand and steered

me down through the first aisle of tombs. Not one had been spared the onslaught of destruction. He stopped and perched on the side of one of the lower tombs.

"Looking around at this, I'm guessing it's the work of teenagers. These aren't political slogans. They're meant to shock in the way that teenagers often do."

I was thinking this over when a macho-sized black cat appeared around the corner of the tomb. He padded up to us sniffing the air. He made straight for me and rubbed himself against my leg. I stroked him and he buried his head in my palm.

"Hey, puss," I said. "Where did you come from?"

He broke off his purring salutation and sat back on his haunches looking up at Felix and me. "I'm the rat-catcher for the cemetery. My name's Zuzu. It's my job to kill the rats and snakes and make the cemetery safe for the citizens of Beaucoup-sur-Mer. I heard you talking and so you must be a witch?"

I nodded. "I am. My friend Felix is a supernatural, a feline like you."

Zuzu edged backwards. "A shape shifter? I've never met one before."

Felix leaned down and touched paws with the member of the smaller branch of his animal tree. "No need to be fearful. We're on the same side, aren't we?"

Zuzu let out a quick meow of confirmation.

"Did you see the rascals who did this damage?" Felix asked.

"I watched them from afar. I'm only a cat. I couldn't stop them. When youngsters like that get together and go rogue, the wise cat keeps away."

"So you wouldn't be able to identify them?"

The cat shook his head, glancing up the slope as he did so. "Watch out. The authorities are here."

He slunk off round the corner and crouched down out of sight.

Dubois had arrived with Father Pedro, Dubois smart in his inspector's uniform complete with revolver, and Father Pedro in his off-duty uniform of jeans and hoodie. Felix and I hurried over to meet them as they entered the elaborate gateway of twin pillars of cut limestone with a canal tiled roof above. Even its pillars were covered in paint. Lamy joined us.

Dubois held out his hand to Felix and bussed me on both cheeks. "Well, here we are: Church and State and Visitors. All set to sort this mess out. Is this as you found things this morning?" he asked Lamy.

"No, Inspector. The vandals left their empty aerosols behind and several dozen empty beer cans."

"You didn't touch them, did you?"

Lamy shifted uncomfortably from foot to foot as the point of Dubois's question struck home. "I'm sorry, Inspector. My first thought was to clear up as soon as possible. It wasn't until after I'd rung Father Pedro here that I thought about fingerprints and DNA. I'm a simple gardener."

Father Pedro stepped forwards and put his arm around Lamy's shoulders in a parochial man hug. "It's all right, Pierre. We know you were doing your best. Now, do you by any chance still have the garbage you collected?"

Lamy's face brightened. "Yes, Father. In the yellow bin just outside the walls. It won't be emptied until next Friday."

"We might be lucky, Dubois," said Felix. "Penzi has friends on the inside of the lab in Cognac. She'll probably be able to get them to work over the weekend to see if they can process the cans for forensic evidence."

Dubois's eyes lit up and then dulled again. "But if the culprits are teenagers, we won't have their fingerprints or DNA on record. We can't ask every teenager in Beaucoup-sur-Mer to give us their prints and a DNA sample, not for vandalism. It would be difficult enough for a murder or a rape."

I glanced around me and back at Lamy and Father Pedro. "It's a pity no one thought to have a CCTV camera installed."

"Mea culpa," said Father Pedro. "I never thought it would be necessary."

Lamy burst in. "But we did. The last mayor insisted on it."

"So, where is it?" asked Dubois.

"We're standing right underneath it," Lamy answered pointing up to the corner of the roof over the gateway.

We all followed his finger, our hearts lifting only to sink again when we noticed the lens had been spray painted.

"They didn't miss a trick, did they?" said Father Pedro. "You just wait until I get them in my church. I'll give them such a penance they'll never even touch a can of paint again."

Dubois laughed. "We have to catch them first."

He walked around the gate and backed slowly keeping his eyes on the camera. He stopped and said, "They would have had to enter the cemetery before they sprayed the lens. Someone will be on the recording, maybe more than the person who put the camera out of action. Where are the recordings kept, Lamy?"

"Outside the cemetery in a metal box next to the

junction box for the telephone system for the area. Here, let me show you."

He led the way out through the gate to a metal container about eight feet tall outside the walls. On the far side stood a box of about the size of a shoe trunk. He unlocked it and carefully removed the disk which he passed to Dubois.

"There you are, Inspector."

Dubois took it from him and slipped it into a plastic evidence bag.

"It occurs to me," he said, "that if we can identify these youngsters, we can trade off their immunity from arrest against their fathers working to clean up the cemetery."

"Why can't we make the teenagers do it?" I asked.

"Dubois is probably thinking along the same lines as I am, boss," said Felix. "We're going to need power tools for this job. We can't ask teenagers to use power tools without lessons in their use and in safety, and we don't have the time for that. And some of them may be too slight of body to handle powerful tools."

I raised my eyebrows at him. "Explain."

Dubois broke in. "Look around you, Penzi. Most of the tombs and vaults are built of cut limestone. The quickest way to get the paint of the tailored stone is to sand it with a disk sander. If the job was any bigger, we'd have to use a sandblaster, but then we'd have to clear up the sand. That's both expensive and time-consuming. We could make the parents pay but we can't buy time."

"And what about the perimeter walls with the rough mortar?"

"We'll have to power wash those. So, you see we need to get the parents on side."

"Where do we go from here then?" I asked.

"I'll rush this recording back to the *gendarmerie*. The sooner we identify at least one of these rascals the better, so we can trace the parents. Penzi, I suggest you and Felix take the cans to your friends in Cognac so we can be prepared with the evidence if this case turns out to be more complicated than it seems at first; if the perpetrators were not local youths."

"And me?" asked Lamy.

"You're doing fine. Carry on with the routine maintenance ready for *La Toussaint* on Wednesday," said Dubois.

Dubois hurried off calling back over his shoulder, "Give me a ring when you're back in Beaucoup, Penzi, and we'll see where to go from there. And I'll take Father Pedro home on my way."

Lamy gave us a black bin bag. Felix and I spent a dirty ten minutes picking the aerosols and empty beer cans out of the bin full of dead flowers and old flowerpots. Then we sped off for Cognac to see Diane Cordier, the pathologist we'd met on one of our previous cases.

3

———

Diane's son asked us where Jimbo was. They'd made friends on our last case. I had to explain that we were on urgent police business. Diane took the sack of tins from us and said she'd be happy to work over the weekend but she had no one to look after her son, Jean.

"Why doesn't he come and spend the weekend with us?" I asked. "Jimbo would love to have some company especially as Felix and I'll be busy."

"Great!" Jean shouted with glee and dashed off to pack a bag.

We wasted no time putting him in the back seat and haring off back to Beaucoup-sur-Mer. Felix called Dubois on the way.

"That's good," Felix said. "Well, better than nothing. I'll tell Penzi."

He swiped his call off.

"So?" I asked.

Felix had the annoying habit of keeping me waiting for news.

"Two young lads show up on the recording, but no one in the *gendarmerie* knows who they are."

"Blow," I said thumping my hand on the steering wheel.

"Dubois says he can organize a door-to-door inquiry with print-outs of the two youths on the recording."

"That'll take forever. We have to find their parents. Organize a work party. Borrow or buy the necessary tools. There has to be a quicker way to find them."

All the way back to Beaucoup-sur-Mer I turned the problem over in my mind. It wasn't until after I'd handed Jean over to Gwinny and a thrilled-to-bits Jimbo that my other brother Sam came into the kitchen to tell us he was going over to the Bonhomie house to spend Saturday evening with Emmanuelle.

"That's it," I said.

"What?" they all asked looking at me.

"The kids who vandalized the cemetery must go to the local high school. Emmanuelle was a pupil there last year, a star pupil, wasn't she?"

Sam nodded.

"It would be awkward to disturb the head teacher on a Saturday evening, but he or she'd probably be receptive to a request from Emmanuelle."

"For what?" asked Sam.

Felix and I explained what had happened and how urgent it was to get the cemetery cleaned up before *La Toussaint* the following Wednesday. We told him how Dubois had photos of two of the vandals but that he hadn't been able to identify them.

"The head teacher will know who they are if they go to the local high school. It's worth a try."

Sam pulled a face. "But we've already arranged for a gang of friends to come round."

Time for my big sister act.

"Sam, this is very important for the community. Emmanuelle's father as mayor of the town stands to lose considerable face over this. It may even cost him the next election. I'm sure if you explain to Emmanuelle how serious this is, she and your friends will be agreeable to my plan."

"All right," he agreed. "Can you come with me to explain? She can phone the head teacher from her house."

"Of course. Felix can call Dubois on the way and tell him what we're planning."

"Shouldn't I ask him to meet us at the head teacher's house?" asked Felix.

"Not until we know he or she's in tonight. Come, let's go. We have no time to waste."

LUCK WENT our way all evening. Emmanuelle found the head teacher at home, a Madame Sablon, and she was happy to oblige. We phoned Dubois to meet us at her house. Madame Sablon had no trouble identifying the two boys concerned, saying they were in the fourth year, a pair of scallywags who mucked about in class.

"I'm not a bit surprised," she said. "I only hope they didn't inveigle any of our good pupils into their silly game. We won't know until you've questioned them, will we, Inspector?" she asked Dubois.

"How are you going to get over their gang loyalty, Inspector?" I asked Dubois. "You're not going to find it easy to persuade them to give up their friends."

"I'll tell them I'll send a team of gendarmes to the houses of all the boys in their class to ask for permission for DNA swabs and fingerprints. I'm sure most of the parents will agree. That's the stick. And for the carrot, I'll tell them that if all the culprits are identified, I'll give their parents the chance to clean up the cemetery in exchange for dropping charges."

"Can you do that?"

"I can bluff, Penzi. They won't want the whole town knowing what they've done once I explain their actions in a negative light."

Madame Sablon agreed. "Boys of that age often get carried away with a dare and regret it afterwards. Offering them a way out at this holy time of the year when we should all be showing respect for those who've gone before us is a good idea."

We made our way home, leaving Dubois to return to the *gendarmerie* and try out his plan on the two lads who would be brought in for questioning. There wasn't much more we could do that night, and we had Diane's son to entertain.

NEXT MORNING, Sunday, Dubois phoned to say he had the full list of the teenage vandals. Father Pedro and Pierre Lamy were organizing the fathers of the boys into a clean-up team. All in all, nine boys had been involved. Three fathers were to power hose the walls and six sand off the paint on the cut limestone of the tombs and vaults. A nasty dusty job. Fortunately, the DIY shops were open for a couple of hours on a Sunday morning, so the parents without the necessary equipment could stock up. The work was to commence at one o'clock after lunch.

"Those poor fathers," said Felix when I gave him the news. "They've been working hard all week, looking forward to their day off, and now they have to make good their sons' lack of civic spirit."

"It does mean we can let Diane know she doesn't have to continue with her forensic tests."

Felix didn't agree. "No, let her continue. You never know what's going to turn up."

I was to remember that later on when we received a second urgent call from Pierre Lamy on the Monday evening. Until then, Felix and I spent a quiet day with Gwinny, Jimbo and Jean, taking the dogs for a long walk along the cliff tops in the afternoon. On the Sunday evening we drove Diane's son home passing the cemetery on our way. Of course, we stopped to have a look at the progress they'd made. They were still all at work in the approaching dusk.

Father Pedro manned a refreshment point, handing out can after can of cheap supermarket beer to wash down the dust. He explained to me that it gets everywhere even when you wear a mask. The fathers switched off their power tools one after the other when they noticed us and gathered round for a great shaking of dusty dirty hands. We told them how impressed we were with their achievement so far.

"We'll be finished in time," said Father Pedro waving his arm to show that the first half of the graves were now pristine.

"Such a terrible thing to do," said one of the fathers. "I am so ashamed of my son."

"Don't be," I said. "Inspector Dubois told me Father Pedro is arranging for all the boys to do community service to make up for their lapse in judgment and for making you, their fathers, work on a Sunday."

"Is that right, Father?" asked the man again.

Father Pedro nodded. "My garden needs some work

and all the church windows could do with a good clean beyond the routine wipe down. That'll keep them out of mischief for a while."

We said goodbye and left them packing away their tools for the night.

"I called in some favors," Diane told us when we dropped her son off. "Three of us worked on the samples today and got through the lot. Now we have to wait for the DNA results. Do you want me to send them to Inspector Dubois when they're available?"

"Please. And thank you. Anything we can do for you, just let us know," I promised.

She gave me a hug saying, "I can never repay you for what you did for the de Portemorency family."

4

————

With no appointments on the Monday, Felix and I gave ourselves over to working in the *brocante* as we usually did when we had a free day. The *brocante* was the soon-to-be shop next door to our house of *Les Dragons* right at the end of the left-hand arm of the crescent making up the bay at Beaucoup-sur-Mer. My father had expressed the wish that we should run an antiques business from the premises, a *brocante* being somewhere between a bric-à-brac store and a serious antiques shop. When we arrived in Beaucoup-sur-Mer the year before, we'd found the place stocked to the ceiling with precious objects and rack after rack of paintings, and junk. We'd cleared out the junk and sorted out the rest of the stock but still awaited a visit from an art expert to value the paintings.

Our friend Izzy Tointon, an American A-list movie star, had promised to arrange for one of her friends, an art restorer at the Louvre, to visit us when he had a spare couple of days. Izzy and her husband had bought the medieval Château Briand, a short way up the north coast. She'd zoomed into our lives in a smart little red sports car, trailed by her ex-SBS bodyguard, Garth. She'd called on us to find a mirror to replace one that had been smashed during a party at the château.

I was remembering the day we'd met when Felix and I entered the *brocante* on the Monday morning. As we walked down the corridor between the tables of objets d'art and the paintings stacked up against the wall, we passed a large mirror. The sight of it hit me in the solar plexus like a hammer and I stopped abruptly making Felix who was behind me slam into me.

"What the hell, boss?" he cried out as I staggered forwards from the impact and fell to the floor on my knees.

He tried to pull me up, but I begged to be able to get my breath back. I was sure I had a cracked rib. At last, I could breathe again and held out my hand for Felix to tug me to my feet.

He reached his arms around me to give me a friendly hug and I let out a yelp.

"Why did you stop so suddenly, Penzi? I could have seriously hurt you... or broken my nose."

I pointed with a shaky finger at the mirror leaning against the wall. "That's what's wrong."

Felix took a step towards it and ran his hands over it. "What this old door? What's wrong with it?"

"Everything. Don't you remember?"

Felix frowned as he tried to understand my panic. Then he shrugged his shoulders as if to say comprehension was beyond him; I had to be mad.

But I wasn't. I was able to see a mirror, but Felix wasn't. To him the mirror was an old door. He couldn't see the heavily gilded cherry wood frame nor appreciate the depth of the beveling. That was how it had been the day we met Izzy. In the ensuing weeks I'd received several unpleasant visits from the witchdoctor of the Wazini, who were a tribe living in the Middle Congo from whence Felix came. The witchdoctor had formed a group of cannibals who dressed in leopard skins, known as the Leopardmen. He was after me because my father, Sir Archibald Munro, had been helping the government to track down and wipe out these vicious murderers.

When I'd told Felix about the mirror, he'd listened to me but still couldn't see the mirror for himself. We'd decided it could be a magic portal although we'd had no proof. I'd laid a spell on it with rosemary and basil to keep the witchdoctor out. However, if that was his point of ingress into our house, it hadn't worked or he'd found a new way in.

Seeing the mirror again had given me the heebie-jeebies.

I stretched out my hand to test it. The surface was icy cold to my fingers, but I pushed my hand on through up to the wrist. The surface rippled around my skin and my hand disappeared from view. I snatched my hand back quickly unsure of what would happen if the rest of me followed it through the mirror.

I held my hand out to Felix saying, "Feel how cold my fingers are. My hand went right through the glass."

Felix grunted an acknowledgement and rubbed my hand between his palms to warm mine up. He didn't say anything for a while.

When my hand was warmed up, he slipped it into his pocket and held it there. "Boss, I never doubted you and seeing is believing. We always did think it was magic."

I'd forgotten all about the strange mirror in the rush of our lives and all the murder cases we'd solved since then.

"What should we do about it?" I asked. "It gives me the creeps."

"It's leaned there up against the wall quite happily for the last year. We could forget about it and get on with our lives."

"How about my finding out if I can pass right through the mirror and out onto the other side? I could have a look around and report back to you."

"Absolutely not, boss. You're not going anywhere without me to keep you safe. All the hobgoblins and spooks of Halloween could be in there. And you know how you hate Halloween."

That made me laugh. "But I can't ignore it now that I've rediscovered it. We have to do something, but what?"

"Let's go back to the house and think about this while we have a cup of tea," Felix suggested.

Sometimes I think he's more English than I am.

BACK IN THE HOUSE, we had tea and cookies with Gwinny in the kitchen where she was busy with her weekly baking session. Jimbo was with her so we couldn't mention the mirror/doorway or whatever it was. The fortnight over *La Toussaint* was a holiday off school for all children in France.

I told Gwinny I needed her advice about something and drew her into the study with Felix and me. Gwinny was also a white witch though she hadn't been an active one for several years. I found her experience and knowledge useful from time to time as I was at such an early stage of my apprenticeship.

Gwinny wiped her floury hands on her apron, pulled out a chair and sat down. "What's so important, Penzi?"

"You remember I found a mirror in the *brocante* last year when Izzy was here? A large mirror, door-sized. That's the problem. To me it's a mirror, but to Felix it's nothing but a door. You couldn't see it as a mirror either. Well, today it spooked me when I saw it. I put my hand through the glass. The surface parted and reformed around my hand in a viscous surge. It defies the laws of physics."

Gwinny nodded slowly. "Yes, I remember you told me about it and it was merely a door to me. We decided it was probably a magic portal to other dimensions, didn't we? A portal through which other supernaturals could pass."

"That's why I put a spell on it," I said.

"What sort of spell?"

"One to prevent it being used as access to the house. Felix and I thought the witchdoctor was getting in that way," I said without thinking.

Gwinny flinched. "What?" she asked. "You never told me he'd been back again."

"You'll have to tell your mother what the witchdoctor's been up to, boss," said Felix.

5

———————

Gwinny had flinched at the mention of the witchdoctor. What did she know about him that she hadn't told us?

As I've mentioned, a few months before, I'd been plagued by nocturnal visits from a supernatural, a witchdoctor. He'd traveled by magic all the way from the Middle Congo. He'd tried to kill me several times by direct attack, and he'd set a huge black cobra on me. My protective aura had held and his attacks had been repulsed. When I reported the events to the High Council of the Guild of White Witches, the chief witch had given me access to a higher level spell to increase the efficacy of my aura, until such time as the High Council could deal with this evil man. However, we'd forgotten to ask the High Council for help to increase the potency of the barrier effect on the mirror portal.

Either the spell I'd placed on the portal was too weak to bar the witchdoctor, or he hadn't been using it at all because he'd visited me again after I'd cast the spell.

I recounted these happenings to Gwinny emphasizing

the wickedness of the man: that he'd appeared draped in the very leopard skin he'd flayed off the body of Felix's mother when he'd ambushed her out in the jungle in the Middle Congo.

"Archie warned me about him years ago," Gwinny began.

Archie was my father, Sir Archibald Munro, world famous anthropologist who'd disappeared and was presumed dead, eaten by cannibals in Africa, the cannibals being of the Wazini tribe. The witchdoctor was their leader. He'd been attempting to bring the whole area under his power, using intimidation as his weapon of choice. My father had been helping the legitimate government against the witchdoctor's Leopardmen, who killed and ate the opposition in a bid to take their victims' life force and add it to their own.

Gwinny was still talking. "If the witchdoctor came here, he must have been on a mission of vengeance to get you, Archie's oldest child."

"That's what the High Council of the Guild of White Witches told me," I said. "So what about this mirror, or portal, or whatever? What should we do? Do you have any advice to give me?"

Gwinny looked from me to Felix and back again with a look of puzzlement on her face. "But what can I tell you that you don't already know?"

"I want to go through the mirror and explore. Find out what's on the other side. Put our misgivings to rest," I said.

Felix shuffled his feet before sitting down. "I can't... won't... let Penzi go alone. It's much too dangerous. The witchdoctor could be lying in wait on the other side of the portal. And then what?"

"So go with her," Gwinny said rising to her feet. "I have to get back to my baking. My angel cakes will be burning."

Felix stood up again in a hurry and caught hold of Gwinny's arm. "I need your help. To me the portal is an old wooden door. When I touch it, it's nothing but wood. There's no way I can pass through with Penzi and keep her safe."

"She has her aura to do that," said Gwinny trying to pull her arm away from Felix.

"Gwinny, what's wrong with you?" I cried out, finding it difficult to grasp the notion that my mother was walking out on me again just as she had all those years ago.

Her knees buckled. She fell to the carpet in a disjointed heap and burst into tears.

I rushed to her and knelt down beside her, wrapped her in my arms and rocked her to and fro until she stopped weeping.

She raised her head to meet my eyes. "Penzi, I'm so sorry. I'm terrified of anything to do with that evil creature."

"Why? What happened?"

She wiped her eyes. "He came for me in London. When we lived in Notting Hill Gate. Archie was in Africa and I was on my own with you three children. I managed to keep him out of the house with help from the High Council of the Guild of White Witches."

"Why didn't you tell me?" I asked, appalled that my mother had been in such danger and I'd not known.

"How could I? It all involved the world of magic. You didn't want to know. Even as a young child you turned your back on everything I tried to teach you."

It was true that my mother and I hadn't had a good mother and daughter relationship. From my viewpoint as a child and a teenager, the rift had been caused by her lack of acceptance of my disability, my dyslexia. Looking back, I supposed she had taken me for stubborn when I refused to learn the *Book of Spells*.

With a new understanding, I asked her, "Is that why you left us? Because you were afraid of the witchdoctor?"

"Partly. It was also because Archie and I were no longer a couple."

"But you left us to the witchdoctor's mercy. How could you do that?"

Gwinny began to sniffle again. She wiped her nose on her apron and said, "Penzi, not everyone in the world is as courageous as you are. Some of us are weak, fragile even. I'm not a warrior. I'm a nurturer."

The thought that she hadn't done much nurturing of us for seven years passed through my mind but I brushed it away. She had been trying to make up for that since she'd come back into our lives in Beaucoup-sur-Mer.

"And I wasn't all bad," she went on. "I arranged with the High Council of the Guild of White Witches for them to ring the house with a protective shield against any future visits by the witchdoctor. And it worked, didn't it?"

Felix gave Gwinny his hand and helped her to her feet. "Come. Sit down and see if you can help us out here."

He led her over to my father's antique leather armchair and she sat down. When I saw that her feet didn't touch the ground, a surge of compassion passed through me. I was from a newer generation, larger and taller physically, more worldly-wise and less dependent than hers. I'd had the advantages of education and social standing that she hadn't as a young girl. Time to show empathy and not criticism.

I gave her a quick hug and passed her the box of tissues to mop up her tears.

"So, can you help us? I want to make sure that the portal

is not a weak spot in our defenses. I need to check out what's on the other side of the mirror. And Felix has to come with me. How can he do that?"

Gwinny blew her nose. She bent her head and twiddled her fingers in her floury apron while she thought.

She looked up at last. "I have an idea, but I want to check it in the *Book of—*"

I was out of the door before I heard the last word. My mother's grimoire had been passed down to me by my father. I kept it in an antique Chinese box in my bedroom.

I raced upstairs. As quick as could be I was back, skittering into the study with the antique red leather tome held tightly in my arms. As I laid it carefully on my father's desk, my mother gasped in wonder.

"I'd forgotten how beautiful it was," she said. "So ornate and elaborate."

Precious gems of all the colors of the rainbow inlaid the cover. As I flipped the cover open, the rainbow combined into a blinding prism of light.

My mother cried out, "Ouch! I always forget that bit."

Felix and I had shielded our eyes in time. I felt bad that I hadn't warned Gwinny. She blinked rapidly several times to soothe her eyes before bending over the book and gently slipping her fingers under one stiff parchment page after the other until she reached the index. Felix watched her in awe. Because he wasn't a witch, he was unable to touch the book or leaf through its pages without receiving an electric shock.

Gwinny ran her finger down the items, stopping now and then and turning back to the relevant page, before shaking her head and returning to the index. Felix and I waited patiently as the brightly colored illuminations flipped backwards and forwards before our eyes. So much ancient wisdom.

"Right," Gwinny said at last. "I've checked it up. There's a simple spell you can use. It doesn't require any special ingredients or complicated words and symbols. All it demands is your heartfelt confidence in the person you choose to accompany you."

Felix nudged me. "I hope you have that, Penzi. Otherwise we're wasting our time here."

Gwinny tutted. "This is no time for joking, Felix. If this mirror is the witchdoctor's way into our house, the sooner you find out and deal with it the better."

Felix rolled his eyes at me but he did stand up straighter.

I walked around to Gwinny and peered over her shoulder at the open page. Of course, I couldn't read what was written there, but I still wanted to have a look.

Gwinny slammed the book closed. "Don't crowd me, Penzi," she said. "Give me the space to explain."

I stepped back and leaned against the desk. Gwinny was breathing heavily. This affair was costing her in ways I didn't understand.

"Penzi," she began at last. "You do promise me you'll be careful?"

"Of course she will," Felix interrupted. "And she'll have me to protect her."

"The witchdoctor's magic is powerful. Black magic can be as challenging as white magic. If he's skulking away somewhere behind that mirror, he won't hold back if Penzi intrudes on his territory."

"Your concern for your daughter does you credit, Gwinny, but we're hardened in the battle against evil, Penzi and I. We won't underestimate the danger. Now please tell us what we have to do, or I'll be dead from impatience and frustration before we even start on this adventure."

Gwinny turned to me. "You have your utmost confidence in this man? You trust him absolutely?"

"Yes, I do. We're work colleagues and friends. We've trusted each other with our lives in the past. And you know him well. He's been living with us for more than a year now."

Gwinny rose from her seat and came towards me, pulling me off the desk and taking my left hand in hers.

"Come here and join us, Felix."

When Felix stood close up beside me, Gwinny laid my hand on his heart.

"Feel his heart beat, Penzi. Tell me when your pulse synchronizes with his."

I wrapped my other hand round my wrist, middle finger on my pulse and waited. Felix and I stared into each other's eyes. His pulse slowed, mine increased until they matched, beat for beat.

"Now," I whispered to Gwinny.

"Keep that going and call out *Felix, vade mecum!*" Gwinny instructed.

Felix blinked to say he was ready.

I called out, "*Felix, vade mecum!*"

A jolt of power ran from his heart up my arm to my own heart. I jumped back.

"Did you feel that, Felix?" I asked my breath coming in gasps.

Felix had gone white, and he'd clapped his hands over his heart.

All he said was, "Wow! That was powerful. What does it mean?"

"It's quite simple, Felix," I said once I'd got my breath back. "It simply means *Felix, go with me.*"

"It's the connection between you that makes it so

powerful," said Gwinny. "I should add that you can only accompany Penzi when she wants you to. She can go to the bathroom on her own."

That made the three of us laugh.

"Thanks, Gwinny," I said. "We'll let you get back to your baking now."

"So, are we on for this adventure?" asked Felix as soon as the door had closed behind my mother.

"Sorting out the *brocante* can wait. I don't feel comfortable now I've remembered about the portal. It's true the witchdoctor hasn't paid me a visit for some time now, but my skin crept with goose bumps when I saw the mirror again today. I can't believe he's given up. I bet he's working on some way to breach my protection."

"Boss, you could be right. Let's put your mind at rest."

We collected up flashlights, cameras and snacks and made our way back to the *brocante* and the mysterious portal.

6

___

"You're sure about this?" asked Felix when they two of us reached the mirror again.

"*Absolument*, as Monsieur Bonhomie would say. But Gwinny didn't tell us how long the *vade mecum* lasts. Do we need to do it again?"

"Better safe than sorry," said Felix in that clipped way of his. "Okay. Time to synchronize our heartbeats," he said taking a couple of slow deep breaths to slow down his pulse.

I wrapped my right hand round my left wrist with my middle finger on my pulse and positioned my left hand on Felix's heart. As soon as our hearts beat as one, I called out, "*Felix, vade mecum!*"

We jumped apart as the surge of power traveled between our hearts.

Felix chuckled. "That's powerful muti. So, who's going first?"

"We'll go together. We can manage it if we squash up tight."

Felix put his left arm round me saying he needed his right arm free in case he had to defend us. I clung on to his waist with my right arm. We led our way with our police-style flashlights in our free hands, pushing them into the glass which gave way and sucked us through into a space as dark as a sunless universe.

Felix had his light on before mine. I was too busy holding onto him to think about switching mine on. There's a lot to be said for having a strong well-muscled man-cum-leopard with you in such spooky circumstances.

As he shone his light around, we discovered we were standing at the top of a flight of stone steps leading down into the bowels of the earth. Felix insisted on leading our descent with me following along behind holding onto the hem of his T-shirt. When we reached the bottom Felix craned his head around the wall.

"No one here," he said pulling me after him.

We stepped off into a vast subterranean chamber. It appeared to be a natural cave in the limestone and not man-made, but that was where natural stopped and strange began.

"Goodness," said Felix. "It's an underground laboratory."

"More like an alchemist's den," I said as I surveyed the test tubes, pipettes and other scientific gadgets whose names I didn't know, science not being my strong point.

"Let's take a quick gander," said Felix striding off down the length of the tables leaving me trailing along behind like a man in a dress shop.

I wiped my hand along the surface of the work tables. No dust. I scuffed my shoe on the stone floor. Again no dust. The place was spotless.

"Felix, I called out. I'm getting a nasty three-bears feeling. Someone's been in here recently."

"I'd say so. No porridge but look, this milk's fresh," he said picking up a cardboard carton and giving it a sniff.

"Who or what has been in here? Could it be the witchdoctor?" I asked, shivering at the thought.

Felix walked back up the line of work tables stopping to examine the utensils and other paraphernalia. "I can't make sense of the work being done here. Look at this," he said picking up a large mortar bowl and tapping it with the pestle which had lain beside it. He put it back on the table and dipped his finger inside. "And what's this substance? They've been grinding something up, but what?"

He picked up a little and rubbed the powder between his finger and thumb. "It's a little gritty, not uniform."

He sniffed his fingers as only a leopard can sniff, sensing out every last little particle of the odor.

"It can't be," he said.

"Can't be what?" I asked bending down to pick up a long white bone I'd noticed at that moment on the floor under the table. I brandished it at Felix.

"Look. I've found a dog bone."

Felix dusted his hand off quickly against his jeans and reached for the bone. He turned it around in his hands and smelled it.

"Just as I thought, boss. It's human. It's someone's femur."

"That's a thigh bone, right?"

"Afraid so. Someone's been grinding up human bones. That can only be one person that I can think of."

"The evil witchdoctor?"

"I thought I detected a familiar smell when we stepped into this ghoul's den. Let me check the cupboard over there."

In four strides, he had the door open and a nasty stink of rotting flesh invaded the chamber.

"Come and see," he said.

There, hanging on a rail, was a tatty leopard skin. Not properly cured by the slimy look and pong of it.

So, it had to be the witchdoctor's lair. He was a magician of a high order, a force for evil but powerful, nevertheless. And he wore leopard skins. Felix had told me that his followers, the Leopardmen of the Wazini, dressed up as leopards to terrify the local inhabitants whom they killed and ate.

My knees gave way and I crumpled to the stone floor banging my coccyx and letting out a yelp of pain. Felix ran to my side and helped me to my feet again.

"Give yourself a minute, boss. Take some deep breaths," he coaxed me.

I drew the odorous air down into my lungs.

"Felix, this noxious atmosphere is doing me no good. Let's get out of here and think things through. I'm afraid I'm going to be sick."

We made it back up the stone steps to the *brocante* with Felix pushing me from behind.

"Phew!" I said as we reached our safe and friendly family kitchen. "That was disgusting and terrifying all at the same time."

"What was?" asked Gwinny turning round from chopping up vegetables for soup.

"Where's Jimbo?"

"He's in his room playing a game on his computer," she answered.

"Just as well," I answered as I collapsed into a chair. "You'll never guess what we found on the other side of the portal."

I must have looked shaken and pale because Gwinny reached for the cognac, poured me a hefty three fingers and held it out to me saying, "Drink this down while I make you a cup of hot sweet tea."

Felix who'd been filling the kettle slotted it into its cradle and switched it on. "Gwinny, it's far worse than anything we could have imagined, but I'll wait until Penzi's got her tea before we tell you about it."

I sipped the cognac, twirling it around on my tongue before swallowing it. I don't usually drink spirits. Although I knew it was to pull me round as they say, I found it hard to swallow neat. In fact, I gave up and passed the glass to Felix asking him to dilute the fiery drink with a splash of water. I resumed my sipping while my mind spun in confusing circles. I was finding out that sometimes the natural and supernatural worlds met in alarming ways, the overlap being like some kind of crazy Venn diagram.

"Well?" asked Gwinny as she placed the mug of hot tea in front of me. "Give."

Felix patted me on the back saying he would tell our story because I needed the sugar boost from drinking my tea.

"Gwinny we've found out that the witchdoctor of the Wazini has been living in a stone chamber underneath the *brocante*. We found signs of recent, very recent, habitation. He's making scientific experiments with human bones. You wouldn't know anything about that from your more extensive knowledge of spells and magic?"

I watched the color drain from my mother's face as she drew out a chair and fell into it. She sat there trembling all over.

"Gwinny?" Felix asked. "Are you all right?"

"Give me some cognac, Felix. The déjà vu has knocked me for six."

She took the glass from Felix and joined me in sipping the restorative liquid slowly, allowing the spirit to work on her body and mind. Poor Felix had to stand and wait until my mother and I had recovered sufficiently to discuss our discovery. In the end he, too, pulled out a chair and sat down with a glass of cognac.

My panic had subsided and Gwinny's color was returning, when my phone rang cutting off any response we might have received from Gwinny. I passed the phone to Felix.

"It's Pierre Lamy, the head gardener for the commune," he whispered in an aside. "He's in a state."

Felix's eyebrows rose as he listened to Lamy and he jerked his head back. It was obviously not good news. He closed the call. Gwinny and I waited for an explanation.

"Someone's stolen the marble plaques off the front of all the tombs and vaults. Not only that, but they've taken the more valuable vases and chalices, the ones relatives use for their cut flower offerings. Some of them are bronze or crystal. A couple are even silver. He wants us to meet him now at the cemetery and help him find the culprit."

I couldn't stop myself from wailing, "Not again? At this time of the day. It'll be dusk soon. I don't want to be creeping about a graveyard after the day we've had. And, anyway, we have our own crisis to deal with."

Gwinny reached across the table for my hand and squeezed it. "Quite right, Penzi. Don't you go."

Should we or shouldn't we? How far should my duty as a white witch be allowed to intrude upon my life as a human being? I weighed up my various responsibilities and added in my own need for mental repose and sleep.

"On a scale of from one to ten, how critical would you judge such thefts?" I asked my mother and my bodyguard.

Felix answered that the time element was critical with *La Toussaint* only thirty-six hours away. However, Gwinny pointed out that the crisis involved theft not danger to life and could wait until the following morning when I'd have had a good night's sleep, and we would have daylight in which to work.

Felix nodded at Gwinny's comment. "True. It'll keep until tomorrow. I'll ring him now."

As Felix made the call, I let out the longest sigh I've ever sighed in my life. Sometimes being a white witch on the side of good demanded too much. This time I was going to put myself first in order to be the better equipped on the morrow to deal with the problem of the cemetery thief. Tonight we had more pressing needs: to discuss the threat of the witchdoctor.

Felix closed his phone down and turned to me. "That's the cemetery problem put on hold for the night. Now, we must consider what to do about the witchdoctor. First of all we must repeat the spell strengthening your protective aura, boss."

When the witchdoctor had first appeared in our house and attacked me, my aura against supernatural attack had not proved strong enough. His magic had managed to dent it and so weaken it. I'd appealed to the High Council of the Guild of White Witches for help and they'd given me special access to a Level Four spell. That had enveloped me in an apricot-colored aura of much greater defensive power. Felix and I had been repeating the spell every month since then to keep up its efficacy.

Felix was being over-protective and I told him so. "I cast the spell two weeks ago. My aura's fine. Isn't it, Gwinny?"

"Stand up," she asked me. "I don't usually notice it; I'm so used to it." She scrutinized me from head to toe. "Felix, it's fine," she said. "A perfect bell shape, no dents, no cracks or creases. It will last another two weeks easily."

The tension that'd had me in its grip since our discovery of the disgusting leopard pelt in the underground chamber of horrors whooshed out of me. I needed an ordinary evening with an ordinary family doing ordinary things. I thrust all thought of the witchdoctor behind the curtain in the back of my mind.

"No more talk of supernatural horrors this evening," I said. "We'll have supper and if you call Jimbo down, Felix, we'll play the Game of Life. He loves that game. It's positive and about families. We'll leave consideration of tomorrow's evil until tomorrow."

7

―――――

We were having breakfast early on the morning of Halloween so we could fulfill our promise to Pierre Lamy to meet him at the cemetery at nine sharp. My phone rang. It was Lamy calling once again in a state of panic. He could barely get his words out.

He calmed a little when I assured him we were on our way and said, "It's worse, much worse, Madame Munro. You must hurry."

I asked him what had happened, but he said he couldn't talk about it on the phone.

"Hurry. Just hurry, please," he finished, ending the call.

"More trouble?" asked Felix.

"Sounds like it. We have to leave now. Immediately."

"But I'm still drinking my coffee, boss," Felix complained.

"It'll keep," I said prying his mug out of his hand and clunking it down on the counter.

As we flew through the front door, Gwinny came down the stairs with Jimbo in tow. "Where are you off to so early?"

"Sorry, can't stop. I'll let you know when we'll be home when I find out what's going on," I called back, hurrying over the cobbled street to the car.

"Where?" Gwinny shouted.

Felix shouted back, "The cemetery."

"Be very, very careful, you two. It's Halloween. There are evil spirits about making mischief."

I was to find out that mischief was an understatement. It certainly seemed so when I drew the car to a stop to see Lamy pacing up and down outside the gate. As soon as he saw us he broke into a run and rushed over, opening my car door before I'd even switched off the engine and applied the hand brake.

"Quick, Madame Munro. You must come and see what I found this morning."

Felix and I followed through the gate into the graveyard. He led us down through the aisles of graves and tombs to the vaults at the far end of the cemetery. The wrought iron gate to the third vault from the left stood ajar.

"In here," he said pushing the gate wide.

It was so gloomy inside after the bright morning sunshine it took my eyes a few moments to adjust, but Felix with his feline capabilities could see in the dark.

I heard him gasp and say, "What's happening here?"

He stretched out his arm towards me, took hold of my hand and drew me close. We were standing beside an ancient stone coffin. Its lid was askew.

"See," said Lamy, pointing a flashlight down into the dark interior.

Expecting to see the shroud or skeleton of a dead body

which had been entombed with all the proper funeral rites, I edged closer and peered down into the space only to jump back with a start. What I could see was a leg, a human leg, covered in flesh. No sign of desiccation.

"Is he alive?" I asked Felix who at that very moment was feeling the temperature of the limb with his forefinger.

He shook his head. "Stone cold. But not long dead from the look of the skin and muscle."

Lamy's hand shook as he held the torch for us.

"Have you checked whether there's a complete body in here?" I asked him.

"No, as soon as I realized the man was dead, I called Inspector Dubois. He should be here any minute with the mayor and Father Pedro. I knew I mustn't touch anything."

"We'd better wait outside," Felix said. "This is a crime scene."

The three of us exited into the bright sunshine of the last day of October and perched ourselves on a nearby tomb while we waited for the authorities to arrive. Felix and I took the opportunity to ask Lamy how he'd discovered the body.

"I have keys to all the vaults. It's part of my job to check they're free of vermin. Yes, we have the cemetery cat who kills the rats and snakes, but the bodies of the rats and snakes have to be removed. And then there's the rat feces. The families are responsible for keeping the vaults clean, so I ring them if necessary to let them know they need to come and clean up."

"And you were checking to give the families time to do some house-cleaning before *La Toussaint*?" I asked him.

Exactly," he answered.

"The vault was locked?" Felix asked.

Lamy nodded.

"Does anyone else have a key?"

"Not that I know of. Only the family and me in each case."

A shiver ran up and down my spine. I wasn't the only person in Beaucoup-sur-Mer who could open locks with magic. Felix grabbed my hand again to warn me not to say anything, as if I would. Sometimes he could be a little overbearing in his role as my protector, but it was obvious from the look on his face that his thoughts matched mine.

What had the witchdoctor been up to now? I had no doubt he was involved.

Felix whispered to me, "I could smell he'd been here, boss. I don't know how we're going to handle this."

"We'll have to play it by ear. If we mention magic and witchdoctors, they'll lock us up."

We were caught in the awkward overlap of the natural and supernatural worlds again.

Felix nudged me. "Shush. Here's Dubois."

As Dubois came striding through the gate and down between the graves to where we awaited him, the mayor drove up with Father Pedro.

"So, what's going on?" asked Dubois. "Nothing good or Madame Munro would not be here."

Lamy nodded. "I called her after I'd called the three of you. I knew this was a difficult situation with *La Toussaint* tomorrow, and she'd been involved with the graffiti problem."

"Quite right," said Dubois giving me a kiss on both cheeks. "How are you, Penzi?"

"Shaken," I replied. "You're not going to like this

Inspector, but Monsieur Lamy here has found a dead body."

"Here?" spluttered Monsieur Bonhomie, the mayor, looking around wildly.

Lamy pointed to the open gate of the vault. "In there, *Monsieur le Maire*. In a stone coffin. I think it's a man."

"You don't know?"

"The lid of the coffin is only partly off to the side. I didn't touch anything and so I haven't looked at the whole body, but the leg on view would seem to be masculine."

"Quite right," said Dubois. "Good man not to have moved anything. I'd better take a look."

Father Pedro stepped forwards. "Has he been dead long? I should administer the Last Rites if he appears to have been dead for less than half an hour."

"I'm sorry, Father," Felix said. "The body's quite cold to the touch."

"Then I can do nothing. His soul is in God's hands," Father Pedro said with a sigh and sat down on the tomb beside us.

Dubois pushed forwards towards the vault. "Come on then, Lamy. Show me what you found."

The two of them disappeared into the spooky opening to return almost immediately.

Dubois rolled his eyes to the heavens. "Couldn't be worse with *La Toussaint* tomorrow."

He walked off to the side. We watched him take out his phone and bark orders for about ten minutes with much Gallic hand waving and foot stamping.

"Right, they're all on the way," he said as he marched back up to us. "The local pathologist is coming, the forensics team from Bordeaux and the local gendarmes. I've said no sirens, no flashing lights and unmarked vehicles. We must do everything we can to keep this quiet and out of the public eye until after *La Toussaint*."

"Perhaps you should have the body sent to Cognac for the autopsy," Felix suggested.

Dubois scowled. "Of course. I've thought of that."

"So, we sit and wait?" I asked. "Or do you want Felix and me to leave, Inspector?"

"No, stay. You should be here for the pathologist's preliminary report." He moved closer to me and whispered in my ear, "I might need to pick your brains later on."

It wouldn't be the first time. Felix and I had helped Dubois solve several murders during our first year in Beaucoup-sur-Mer. Fighting evil in the name of good was part of my job description as a white witch, not that Dubois knew that, of course.

THE TIME DRAGGED on and we all became thirsty. The mayor sent Lamy off to buy us all a coffee and a casse-croûte each, the French for a snack usually half a baguette with filling. I could have done with a glass of red wine, but Monsieur Bonhomie was minding his official reputation so early in the day.

At last Dr Ambrose, the local pathologist, arrived but she had to wait until the forensics turned up. Their work took them another hour and a half.

The team leader came over to us when they'd finished and held out a handful of small bones. "We found these scattered at the back of the vault."

"Let me see," said Dr Ambrose elbowing the rest of us out of the way.

She gloved up and began poking the bones about on the

team leader's palm. She held the bones up one by one to examine them more closely. "They would appear to be human finger bones," she said.

Dubois turned to Lamy. "Have you ever seen bones on the floor of one of the vaults before?"

Lamy shook his head. "Everything's strange today. I've never seen such a bizarre set of circumstances."

I thought bizarre was putting it mildly.

The bones were placed in an evidence bag and handed to the pathologist for confirmation.

"You'd better date them," Dubois added. "This is the most puzzling case. We seem to have bones stolen from a coffin, but then we have a dead body added in to the mix. It doesn't make sense."

"Can I go in and look at the body now?" asked Dr Ambrose.

The forensics man nodded and added that his men had removed the coffin lid. "And there is a whole body in there," he said, "but prepare yourselves for a shock when you see it."

The pathologist picked up her case and entered the vault, accompanied by Felix and me as observers.

The body was that of a malnourished male whose age was hard to tell given the state of his musculature. Probably about thirty-five. He wore dirty shredded jeans, a torn T-shirt and a khaki hoodie. His sneakers were mismatched in color; one black, one gray. He hadn't shaved for a while his skin being ingrained with dirt and sweat. I took him for North African, possibly Libyan.

However, his left sleeve and left trouser leg had been cut away.

"Someone's sliced off his calf muscle and the muscle from his upper arm," said the pathologist putting my thoughts into words while I was still coming to terms with what I saw before me.

"Definitely post mortem," she added. "Now, why would anyone want to do that?"

Felix nudged me. I hadn't been going to say anything. I made a non-committal noise. To Felix and me it was yet another indication that the witchdoctor was involved. He was a cannibal. And the possible bone thief. He had to get the bones we found in his laboratory from somewhere. It was unfortunate for him that he'd picked the week of *La Toussaint* to stock up his larder and laboratory.

All of a sudden my legs gave way and I sank to the cold stone floor of the vault. The horror had hit me right in the core of my being. The man who'd done this was hell-bent on catching and killing me, possibly even planning to eat me to add my magic strength to his.

The pathologist had looked my way at the sound of my fall. "Take her out of here, Felix," she instructed him. "She needs fresh air. This is gruesome for me, and it's my profession."

Felix knelt down beside me and asked if I could walk.

"Just get me out of here," I mumbled. "If I wasn't sitting down, I'd be fainting."

He eased me to my feet and helped me up the steps out into the fresh air.

Dubois came running towards us. "What has happened to Penzi?"

Felix brushed him off. "It's all right. All under control. The sight of the body was too much for her. The flesh on the man's arm and leg has been sliced off."

"Don't," I managed to say as I leaned sideways and vomited up my makeshift lunch.

Monsieur Bonhomie hurried over and thrust his huge pocket handkerchief at me.

"I'm sorry," Felix said to them all. "I have to take Penzi home. This experience has been too much for her."

"But I can call you tonight with news and to ask your thoughts?" asked Dubois.

"Yes, yes," I nodded. "But I have to get away for now."

Felix led me to the car. "Do you feel all right to drive?"

I shook my head and pointed to the passenger door.

"Very well. We'll risk it," Felix said as he closed the door behind me and made his way around to the driver's seat.

Being an illegal immigrant and a Savannah cat at that, one who could shift into a leopard at will, Felix didn't have a driving permit or any valid documentation. For once I didn't care about anything except getting as far away as possible from that promise of what could happen to me if the witchdoctor ever got his way. However, I did spare a thought for the dead man, wondering if he could have been one of the thousands of hopefuls who make their way across the Mediterranean in search of a better life.

WHEN WE ARRIVED back home at *Les Dragons*, Felix carried me upstairs to my bedroom, brought me a cup of hot sweet tea and told everyone I was not to be disturbed. To my amazement, I fell asleep and didn't wake up until teatime.

8

———

I found Gwinny and Felix in the kitchen nattering over a cup of tea and a plate of cookies.

"Where's Jimbo?" I asked.

Gwinny laughed. "You're a sleepyhead. Jimbo's at his school's Halloween party at the Social Center. He was a little upset he didn't get to show off his vampire costume to you. I told him you weren't feeling well, and I'd be collecting him this evening when the fun is over."

Halloween – how that sent shivers running up and down my spine, especially after the day we'd had. All the pretend weirdos seemed like so much fluff after a day spent in a graveyard with a real corpse, one that had bits of its body missing, moreover. I couldn't wait for Halloween to be over.

Felix pushed his chair back and stood up saying to Gwinny, "Forgive us if Penzi and I repair to the study alone. We have something serious to discuss."

"What?" I asked.

Gwinny gave me a funny look. "I'd guess he means the body in the cemetery."

I gasped. "You told Gwinny. But the mayor doesn't want anyone to know about that."

Felix tutted as he thrust my mug of tea into my hand. "Surely Gwinny doesn't count? She's a white witch after all, and we may need her advice."

Gwinny left her seat and stood in front of the kitchen door barring our way out. "My advice is to leave it alone. Have nothing to do with it. You have no idea what you are messing with on this night of all nights."

I pushed her gently out of the way. "Don't worry. I have no intention of ever setting foot in that cemetery again. And Felix does everything he can to stop me from placing myself in danger. You know that."

"Famous last words," she whispered at me as Felix herded me through the door in front of him. "Don't say I didn't warn you."

～

"So what's so important and so confidential that we have to leave Gwinny out of the discussion?" I asked Felix defiantly, as I took my father's old leather armchair and pivoted from side to side.

"We should phone Dubois for the latest news. When we know if he's found anything out, we can discuss the case and our standing in it."

"Felix," I said stopping the swing of my chair and giving him all my attention, "we don't have any standing in the case of the dead body in the vault. That's over as far as we're concerned. It's way beyond my expertise and yours."

"Hush, boss. Let me call Dubois and find out what's what."

I picked up a pen and doodled while Felix put the call

through. His expression remained serious throughout so I deduced Dubois hadn't progressed much.

"Well?" I prompted as Felix put his phone in his pocket.

"The victim had no identification; no ID card, no credit cards, no correspondence, no health card – nothing. No one answering his description is missing. He isn't from around here. The only hit they had was when they tried his fingerprints against those from the cans we cleared up after the youngsters had sprayed graffiti all around the graveyard."

"So he drank a few beers. Has Dubois asked the boys if they saw this man?"

"Yes, and they didn't. Dubois's guessing he's an illegal immigrant, a vagrant."

"Someone no one will miss. Someone with no record. It'll be hard for Dubois to know where to start with no links to anyone. What about cause of death? The flesh was cut off him post mortem according to the pathologist."

"She says he was killed some time yesterday evening, before midnight. She can't pin down the cause of death. If pushed, she says he died of shock; had a heart attack."

I took a deep breath. "Fright at seeing the witchdoctor will do that to you, especially after a few beers. What does Dubois say about motive?"

"It's all conjecture: a serial killer who likes the taste of human flesh. He says the victim made it easy for the killer, being in a deserted place late at night and looking like a tramp."

"Dubois won't have found any clues or forensic evidence. The witchdoctor will have carried out the murder using black magic."

"Correct as to absence of evidence," said Felix. "Dubois

says he's stumped. Wants to know if we'll go in and see him tomorrow."

I considered what Felix had passed on to me. It was an impossible situation for us. We were ninety-nine point five per cent sure we knew who the murderer was: the evil witchdoctor of the Wazini. However, we couldn't tell anyone that. What were we to do?

Felix clicked his fingers in front of my face snapping me back to reality and the problem at hand. "You were lost for a moment there, boss."

"We have a gargantuan problem, Felix. We can't tell Dubois what we know about the murderer." I sighed and went on. "But if we don't say anything, Dubois stands to lose professional credibility because he won't be able to solve the case. Monsieur Bonhomie might lose the next election as mayor. Father Pedro will never know who desecrated the cemetery. And poor Lamy will be frightened to go to work."

"I don't see any way of preventing all that from happening, boss. There's no way we can tell them about the witchdoctor. Can you imagine their faces if we told them this wicked man travels through a wormhole all the way from the Middle Congo; that he's been trying to find you and kill you in revenge for your father's work in stopping the witchdoctor's followers from eating the rest of the Wazini tribe?"

"I agree with you, Felix. We simply can't tell them. This is one time when we can't put everything right, but we could ambush the witchdoctor and liquidate him. It's second best, I know. At least he wouldn't go around killing any more people in our quiet little town."

"And you'd be safe once he's dead." Felix closed his eyes for a couple of minutes. "But," he said when he opened them again and looked across the desk at me, "how do we do it? And, more importantly, how do we keep you safe?"

"We know he can't get through my protective aura now that it's been strengthened. We've seen him try before and fail. You would be in greater danger than me."

"True, but I can look after myself," said Felix flicking his claws out to prove the point.

"Being a leopard didn't save your mother," I reminded him.

"True again, but my mother wasn't a shape shifter. I'm supernatural."

We fell silent while we pondered how to carry out such a dangerous plan.

As if reading my thoughts, Felix said, "Make no mistake about it, boss. It would be a hazardous undertaking, one in which we might not succeed."

"And I don't want to set foot in that cemetery again, especially not on Halloween. I don't know why I'm even considering it."

"Yes, you do. For all the reasons we've mentioned, not forgetting that you're a white witch, and it's your vocation to fight evil."

"It's such a burdensome vocation, Felix," I said, wishing I could be anywhere for the night of Halloween but Beaucoup-sur-Mer with its spooky graveyard.

"Let's run over our defenses: you have your aura; I have my special capabilities as a leopard and as a man. As to attack: what spells could you use?"

"We could try the *freeze* spell."

"Boss, the *freeze* spell is defensive. It only holds him while we escape. We want to take the battle to him this time."

"You mean kill him? I couldn't do that, Felix. However wicked he is it's not in me to kill another human being."

"Penzi, we can't hold him with a citizen's arrest and hand him over to the authorities. He's a magician. You're a witch. Linking the natural and supernatural worlds in that way wouldn't work."

"What is the point of this exercise then, Felix? You've lost me."

"Is there some way we could immobilize him forever? We could use the *freeze* spell for that, but we don't have any idea of how long it lasts."

"And maybe I have to be there to hold it in place?"

"So many unknowns. There's too much trial and error involved at your level of witchcraft, boss, and we'd be playing with our lives here."

I shut my eyes and imagined the cemetery, not that I wanted to, but it might put me in the mood; give me a flash of inspiration.

I had an idea. Obvious really, when you think about it.

"We could turn him to stone. He'd look like one of the statues you see in the vaults."

Felix laughed. "Hardly, boss. Anyone less like an angel I couldn't imagine."

"The vaults are dark. A strange statue right at the back wouldn't be noticeable."

"It's worth a try. Go and fetch your *Book of Spells* while I get us a drink, something stronger than tea is called for."

When I returned Felix had a bottle of pineau, glasses and a bowl of ice on my father's desk. He poured us both a heavy slug and plopped a chunk of ice in each glass. We sipped in silence for a few moments before returning to the project in hand: the permanent elimination of the evil witchdoctor of the Wazini from our lives.

As I'm dyslexic, Felix has special permission from the High Council of the Guild of White Witches to read the spells and teach them to me, but he could not touch the pages for fear of being shocked with a mighty pulse of energy. The *Book of Spells* itself was a magnificent example of magic art. Its vellum pages, adorned with medieval illuminations of startling bright colors even after so many centuries, were bound with an antique red leather cover studded with precious jewels which packed a fearsome power. Knowing this, we both closed our eyes as I opened the cover. The explosion of light triggered by my action as the gems fused into a prism of startling whiteness penetrated through my eyelids and made me jerk even though I'd been expecting it.

"Takes me my surprise every time," said Felix rubbing his eyes.

"To business," I said. "We're running out of time. It'll be dark soon."

As I slid my finger down the leaves of the book and turned them over at Felix's behest, he read down through the index looking for a spell to cause petrification.

His hovering finger halted halfway down the third page. "We'll try this one. Turn to page 111, boss."

I went too far and Felix checked me. I've always found figures particularly difficult to read as there is no context to them in most cases. A few false flips and we were on page 111. Felix read through the spell in silence.

"Well?" I asked growing impatient and anxious about what I'd have to do and the amount of mental energy I'd have to summon to cast the spell.

"Right, boss," Felix said, "it's not difficult but you have to be touching a piece of the stone you want to use. Marble or granite for example."

"We should use limestone. It'll be less conspicuous because most of the statues in the cemetery were limestone; only a few were of marble. So look up the Latin for limestone."

Felix moved over to his laptop and did a search. "Okay, got it. *Calx, calcis.*"

He shut the lid and looked back at the *Book of Spells.* Suddenly, he raised his head and shot me a grave look. "Boss, it is of the utmost importance that you take precautions now—"

In order for a spell not to work I had to cross my fingers.

"—otherwise you'll probably turn me into stone."

So, I crossed my fingers and held them out in front of me to give Felix reassurance that he wouldn't be petrified for eternity.

"Teach me the spell then," I told him.

He explained the symbols I had to hold in my mind while my fingers touched the piece of limestone in my pocket, and he taught me the words I'd have to utter: *Muto te in calcem,* which means *I turn you into limestone.*

"That wasn't difficult. I could probably have worked that out for myself," I said thinking back to Latin 101.

"But not the symbols?" Felix corrected me.

I nodded. Some spells were easy; some like this one were complicated with symbols and words... and to carry a piece of the right kind of stone.

"I need a piece of limestone," I said

"Plenty of that lying around the graveyard. You can pick up a piece there. We should have some supper and put together a basket of food and drinks to take with us, because we could be there all night waiting for the witchdoctor to appear."

"He won't appear in daylight. I don't suppose he'll know anything about what went on today. Can you imagine his face when he finds his victim's body's gone?"

Felix burst into laughter. "That'll be worth crouching in the cold and dark," he said.

9

———

As soon as the sun had slipped below the Atlantic Ocean, Felix and I climbed into our car and drove through the town, out under the medieval town gates and on to the cemetery. Along the way we passed groups of children and adults tricking and treating. Jimbo was still with his school party. I was glad the teachers would be shepherding the kids so that they didn't come to any harm. Much as I hated Halloween, I couldn't spoil Jimbo's fun and keep him in.

When we neared the cemetery, I parked the car some way off behind a clump of bushes, not wanting to announce our presence to the witchdoctor. We walked the rest of the way. Zuzu, the ferocious cemetery cat, met us at the gate.

"I don't have any news to report, Madame Munro," he said. "The police party left at about three o'clock, and no one's been here since, not even any of the townspeople. The nasty man doesn't usually appear until much later."

I explained part of our plan to Zuzu, the part about the ambush not what our full intentions were, saying we'd be hiding in the vault where the body was discovered.

"Do you want me to warn you when the man arrives?" the brave cat asked me.

"It would be helpful, but don't let him see you," I advised him giving him a tickle behind his ears.

"I won't," he said ambling off to hide behind one of the gravestones.

With Felix guiding me over the rough terrain, his arm through mine, we descended the rough path down to the target vault. Felix shielded his flashlight with his other hand. The lack of light made our going difficult. The moon wouldn't be out for several hours on this dark night of all nights in the year's calendar.

We found the gate locked. I used my *unlock* spell to get us in but found the key in the lock on the inside. In all the commotion during the day, Lamy must have forgotten to take it with him. We ducked under the police tape and tiptoed down into the gloom. The moss clinging to the sides of the vault and to the stone coffins exuded a damp unpleasant odor not apparent during the relative warmth of the daytime. The police had slid the lid back on its coffin.

All appeared to be untouched, but the ancient limestone seemed to be holding its breath. A shiver ran down my spine making me break out in a cold sweat. I didn't want to be there. This would be a trial to the death, and I wasn't sure my Level One magic would prevail against the evil magician's Level Thirteen. So much depended upon the surprise of our ambush.

I ducked back outside and collected a piece of limestone which I tucked away in the pocket of my jeans ready for the *petrification* spell should we need it.

I locked the gate behind me again.

"We should crouch down behind that coffin at the back," Felix said, pointing to an ancient sarcophagus adorned with a sculpture of the erstwhile inhabitants who I guessed had long since turned to bone and dust.

Crouching and kneeling on the cold floor for hours took a toll on us both.

"What's the time?" I whispered, although there was no one but ghosts to hear me.

"Half past ten," Felix mouthed at me. He pointed to himself and then to the entrance. "I'm going to wait inside the gate in leopard mode so I can get behind him and cut off his retreat."

He eased his way out from behind the stone edifice adding, "There's not enough room here for me to shift."

Once in the wider space behind the victim's coffin, he inhaled deeply several times. His muscles rippled. Before my eyes, his skin morphed into the rosetted coat of an African leopard, his ears rounded and his long tail thrashed out behind him. He flicked his claws in and out at me in fun and padded across to gate where he sprang up onto the protruding stone lintel above the wrought iron entrance and settled into a leopard's favorite ambush position.

I fingered the piece of stone in my pocket with one hand and crossed the fingers on the other while I ran over the words and symbols of the *petrification* spell.

No sooner was Felix in position crouched on his powerful haunches, than Zuzu burst in through the bars of the gate.

"He's coming," he hissed. "The evil one's climbing out of one of the graves at the top of the cemetery."

"Come and stay by me," I whispered. "It's too late for you to get away now."

Zuzu, for all he was the brave cemetery guard, cowered down next to me shivering from his pointed ears down to the end of his tail which lashed involuntarily from side to side in expression of the apprehension he felt for what was coming.

We heard heavy footsteps and a muttering at the gate. We didn't dare have any light, but the witchdoctor's purulent stench preceded him, identifying him. As he ducked his head and entered the vault, the odor became so overpowering it was hard to breathe. He was in his full witchdoctor garb: necklace of black scorpion skeletons; leopardskins slung around his shoulders and cinched around the waist with a belt of monkey skulls. Nor had he forgotten his war paint of white surrounding his blackened eye sockets. Overall hung the blue aura I remembered.

He clicked his fingers and a purple light appeared hovering in the air above his head. It followed along with him as he shuffled over to the stone coffin in which he'd left his victim the night before.

He stopped suddenly, his features eerily delineated by the strange purple light. He was puzzled; he'd left the lid ajar. He touched the coffin lid as if to verify someone had closed it, then stood back. He spun slowly surveying the interior of the vault. Zuzu and I shrank back out of sight. Satisfied he was alone, the witchdoctor advanced again and bent his knees. The belt of bones around his waist clacked in the silence. Using both hands he pushed hard against the lid sliding it partway across the corner. His eyes narrowed as he peered into the dark space. At first he couldn't believe his eyes. He plunged his hands into the coffin and swept them from side to side searching for his victim in the gloom, but all he found was an age-old skeleton. He grabbed a handful of bones and flung them on the floor of the vault letting out a screech of rage. He threw himself into a wild fit of stamping, grinding the bones to dust beneath his feet.

Zuzu shot out of our hiding place and zoomed up the

steps out into the fresh air, unable to bear the suspense a moment longer.

I expected Felix to launch himself off from the lintel and knock the witchdoctor to the ground so we could drag him to the rear of the vault before turning him into a statue. Why was Felix hesitating?

A low muffled sneeze reached me even as the witchdoctor turned towards the sound. Quick as a flash he waved his arms in the air in Felix's direction and cried out a string of words in an unintelligible dialect. A transparent shield dropped down from the ceiling to the floor with a bump, bounced and held, sealing Felix in against the gate and blocking his access to the witchdoctor... and to me.

Felix jumped anyway, launching himself at the evil magician who stood cackling quietly to himself as Felix crashed into the shield and fell to the ground. Felix picked himself up, scanned our side of the barrier to find me, but I kept down out of the witchdoctor's line of vision. I watched as Felix prowled up and down, up and down, stopping to claw the screen but making no headway at all.

I considered my options: stay in hiding until the magician left and lose our chance to attack him, or leap out and use the *petrification* spell. The trouble was he had to be in my line of sight for the spell to work. I would have to expose myself. Not a problem, I thought, with my special protective aura, but I had to screw up the nerve, and I was terrified.

Deep breaths, Penzi, I told myself. *Deep breaths. Get everything absolutely ready and then spring out and cast the spell.*

The witchdoctor paced up and down the vault, peering here and peering there. Any moment now he would find me. *He who hesitates is lost.* I had to make a move. I took another deep breath to galvanize my muscles, leapt to my feet and edged out from behind the sarcophagus at the very moment the witchdoctor turned my way. Our eyes met: panic and horror filling mine; satisfaction and glee his.

Now. I had to act now. I brought the magic symbols to mind and reached into my pocket. He reached into his and drew out a skin bag distracting me for a fatal second. As my mind scrambled to return to the words of the *petrification* spell, he pulled out a handful of gritty dust and threw it all over my aura. To my horror, everywhere it touched, my aura melted away like nylon torched by a match.

Instinctively, I tried to push the melting substance off me. That was the opening the witchdoctor had aimed for. He darted towards me, grabbed hold of my hands and dragged me towards the stone coffin. Gone was my chance to touch the piece of limestone in my pocket. I was so startled I couldn't think straight, and he was able to bind my hands with an electrical tie. Then I remembered the *freeze* spell. I summoned up the words and symbols and cast the spell, but nothing happened. I tried again. Still nothing.

Now he was unhooking a taser from his snake-skin belt. He burst into a spate of high pitched laughter at my attempts to freeze him. His protection held against my spell. The witchdoctor dumped me on the ground next to the coffin while he slid the top off. He pulled me to my feet again and pointed the taser at me.

I glanced at Felix. He was morphing back into his man state. He'd decided he needed his opposable thumbs. He must have had a plan, but what I didn't know. And that's the last I remembered.

10

———

F *elix*

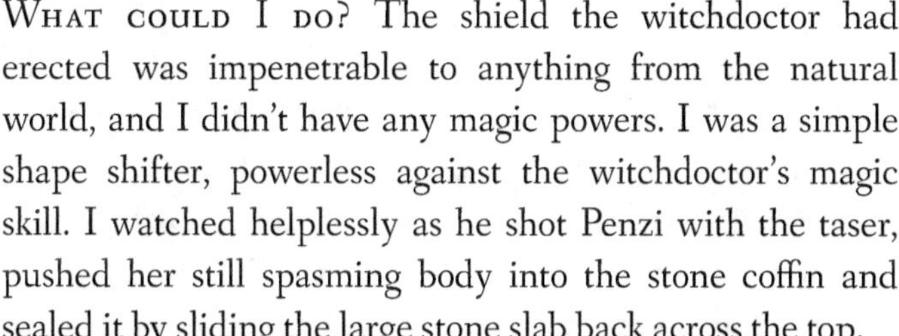

WHAT COULD I DO? The shield the witchdoctor had erected was impenetrable to anything from the natural world, and I didn't have any magic powers. I was a simple shape shifter, powerless against the witchdoctor's magic skill. I watched helplessly as he shot Penzi with the taser, pushed her still spasming body into the stone coffin and sealed it by sliding the large stone slab back across the top.

What was the witchdoctor planning to do? Let her suffocate? Kill her and cut her up? I couldn't hang around unable to do anything and watch her die. I had to do something.

Think, think, I told myself. *What do you know about magic?* Nothing was the answer.

But I knew someone who did.

Gwinny.

I ran up the steps out into the cemetery where a hazy

moon was now shining a pallid light down upon the funeral monuments and gravestones. A trio of bats flew past. A perfect Halloween setting. I pulled out my phone and called Gwinny. It was so good to hear her voice. A human sound in the midst of all the supernatural danger.

I explained the situation and asked for her advice. A couple of seconds passed.

"Is this some kind of sick joke, Felix?" she asked at last. "Because if it is, I suggest you both stop drinking and come home at once before you do something even sillier."

"Gwinny, cross my heart. This is real. The witchdoctor has your daughter in his power. He's erected a magic shield. No human being can get near him. Even I can't. I'm sure he's going to kill her. We don't have any time to lose."

Gwinny didn't answer.

"Gwinny?" I said again.

"I'm thinking."

I waited, aware that every moment could be the beginning of the countdown to Penzi's death.

"Gwinny?" I ventured again.

"Yes, I'm still here. We have to call upon the High Council of the Guild of White Witches. This is too big for me and way above Penzi's level. They have to help Penzi this time."

"You're a witch. You could visit the dolmen and summon them to her aid. There's twenty minutes to go before midnight."

She sighed down the phone at me. "Felix, I can't. I just can't."

"Not even to save Penzi?"

"I'd do anything to help her, but I don't know where the dolmens are here. The last one I visited was years ago and miles away in Brittany. And I'm looking after Jimbo. He's fast asleep upstairs after his Halloween party."

"What about Sam?"

"He's still in Bordeaux with Emmanuelle. I can't leave Jimbo alone."

"Can't you take him with you?"

"How? I don't know the way as I've said. I have no SatNav in my car. No time to find out. No time to risk getting lost. You'll have to go, Felix. It's all up to you."

"But I'm not a witch. Only a white witch can summon the High Council, you know that."

"I'm sure they'll make an exception in this case to save Penzi and get rid of the witchdoctor. He's their responsibility, after all. Just do it, Felix."

"I don't have any of the stuff I need," I pleaded.

"Improvise, man. Improvise. You're a strong intelligent supernatural. You'll think of something," she said and closed the call.

Despair surged through my mind and body, robbing me of what little common sense I had. I sat down heavily on the nearest tomb. Something rubbed against my leg. I looked down to see Zuzu gazing up at me, confidence and trust in his bright yellow eyes.

"We can do it," he said. "And I'm a cat. We're special in the world of witches."

"You heard?"

"Couldn't help it. Hadn't we better get moving if we're to get to this place before midnight?"

I shook myself mentally and physically. Zuzu was right. I was a strong, powerful shape shifter of the leopard tribe. We leopards are known for being the most cunning of all the animals. I could do it.

I scooped Zuzu up in my arms, realizing as I did so that

he was a natural creature, one of the requisites for summoning the High Council. As I hurried up the hill and along the lane towards the car, I thought of the others. Cognac. We'd used my Laphroaig before in a pinch. I could do that again if I had any left. I opened the car door, thrust Zuzu onto the passenger seat and took out my flask and shook it. Good. Half full. What was next? A precious jewel. That stumped me. But not for long. I remembered I'd found Penzi's lost amethyst earring when I cleaned out the car the week before. I'd put it in the ashtray. Good. It was there. Chalice? The ashtray would have to do in an emergency. Matches to light the spirit? I'd found a lighter, too, and wondered at the time if Sam had taken up smoking. So, I had everything except the bay leaves. Zuzu and I would have to try without them.

"Hold on tight," I said to Zuzu as I switched on, put the car in gear, let out the clutch with a whoosh and zoomed off into the blackness of the near approaching Halloween midnight.

On the way I spotted what looked like a bay tree in a garden. I swung into a handbrake turn and snatched a long spray of leaves. I was no witch and certainly no cook. I could only hope I'd made the correct botanical choice.

Minutes later I parked the car at the bottom of the hill. I galloped up the rough terrain to the summit with Zuzu tucked into my jacket. The dolmen, the portal into the world of white magic, lay before us. Two minutes to midnight. I laid the leaves and the earring down on the top stone. I had no idea whether Penzi's earrings were genuine stones or not. I could only hope for the best. I filled the ashtray with the scotch, lit it and as the blue flame spun up into the darkness I hurried three times in a clockwise direction around the altar stone. Remembering at the last second to hide my eyes, I waited for the bright flash that always accompanied the evaporation of the precious gem before opening them again.

I looked up and around me.

Nothing but a spooky clearing on the top of a hill surrounded by ancient trees.

No sign of the High Council.

I hadn't passed the test.

They wouldn't come. Of course, they'd be busy on Halloween.

I'd turned away and was on the point of descending the hill when a voice called out behind me, "It's Mpenzi Munro's friend and helper, isn't it?"

I stopped and spun round. The welcome sight of the High Council of the Guild of White Witches burst upon me, shining and shimmering as they hung above the dolmen in the blackness of a Halloween midnight.

"Your Ladyship," I gasped as I strode the few paces back to the dolmen. "Thank you, oh thank you, for answering my call. We have no time to lose."

"You're here to tell us young Mpenzi is in mortal danger from the black-hearted witchdoctor of the Wazini?"

"The very reason. Will you help us?"

The chief witch beamed down at me with her friendliest smile, surprising me. I'd expected her to be angry at my irregular summons of the High Council.

"No. I'm not annoyed by your actions, Felix. They do you credit. We were on our way to the cemetery when we received your call. Quick as you can, shift into your leopard form and jump up onto the top stone."

I inhaled deeply to pump up my heart and my muscles and made the fastest shift I've ever done, surprising poor Zuzu who meowed loudly as my body changed, my clothes fell away, and he plummeted to the ground. Fortunately, his feline instincts came into play and he landed on all four paws. I gathered him up, bent in a mighty crouch and sprang for the top of the dolmen. Before I'd landed the chief witch had reached down and grabbed hold of my scruff.

"Off we go," she said.

We entered a spinning tunnel of bright white light, all seven witches and me and the cat. A nano-second later the tunnel vanished. Down below us lay the cemetery silent and deadly in the sickly moonlight.

The chief witch told me to return to my ambush position inside the gateway of the vault and to wait without making a sound and without moving an inch, but to be ready when called upon. With that, she let go of my neck and I floated down to the ground with Zuzu clinging to the fur on my back.

Were we in time?

Was Penzi still alive?

I padded forwards and slunk down the steps into the vault. A strange whistling reached me as I descended. The witchdoctor lay stretched out on top of Penzi's stone coffin, snoring in his sleep.

Had he already harmed Penzi and was now sleeping it off?

I couldn't tell. All I could do was watch and wait.

A faint shimmering around the edges of the ceiling of the vault caught my attention. The High Council was there, all seven of them, hovering above the scene, but what were they doing? A high electrical tension built in the vault behind the witchdoctor's shield. Flickers of static bounced and sizzled off the statuary and the limestone walls of the vault.

Something moved in the depths. Something that

reflected the light of the static bursts. Something that rippled.

Out of the shadows slithered the head and first coils of a gigantic serpent, its tongue flicking from side to side as it searched for heat – searched for the living – for prey. I held my breath as it oozed out further into the open space. An African rock python. It was the largest one I'd ever seen, its girth the size of a young girl's waist. Slow and deadly to the unsuspecting – especially the sleeping.

Up above, the seven witches, as lacking in mercy as the witchdoctor down below, held hands and began a low chanting.

The python continued its unstoppable slide along the flagstones at the side of the coffin testing for heat as it went. Satisfied it had found the source of its next meal it raised up its head and flicked its tongue along the length of the witchdoctor as if measuring him.

That's when the doctor woke up from his heavy sleep and sat up. The snake seized its chance, slithering up and around the man's chest: one coil... two... then three. The witchdoctor's screams echoed off the walls. In the gaps while he took a breath, a ghastly crunching could be heard as the python squeezed the life out of him.

If Penzi was still alive, she had to be terrified with the noisy thrashing going on above her. Lucky for her, she wasn't a witness to the slow, powerful and inexorable crushing of the witchdoctor's ribcage and the resulting collapse of his lungs and black heart.

The moment his life force left him, the shield shattered and fell to the floor in front of me.

The snake paused to look up at the High Council high above. The chief witch hesitated for a moment, but then she nodded. Taking that as permission, the great snake began to swallow the witchdoctor's broken body.

I couldn't stay around and watch such an ending, however wicked the witchdoctor had been. I knew from experience it would take at least an hour for the snake to complete its swallow and then hours for it to digest the body. So, I broke silence and dared to address the chief witch.

"Your Ladyship, I'm anxious about Penzi. I can't open the coffin with that huge serpent on top of it. I want to check she's still alive. Furthermore, this is such an inhumane way for a man to be killed however wicked he was; such an undignified ending."

The chief witch was taken aback for a moment, and I expected to be transformed into the proverbial toad, but she turned to her council for a quick conference. They all jabbered away but reached a consensus, nodding their heads in agreement.

The chief witch stretched her hand out in front of her, snapped her fingers and pointed at the writhing muddle on the coffin. She uttered what I took to be more Latin. Instantly, reptile and man vanished. A smoldering pile of black ash took their place.

I rushed forwards and heaved the top off the stone coffin with my powerful fore shoulder. Penzi lay there on her side as she'd fallen in, ancient broken bones all around her.

But was she alive?

11

———

F *elix*

❧

I LEANED into the coffin and bit through the tie binding her wrists. She moaned and shifted slightly in involuntary relief. Then her eyes opened, and she saw me staring down at her.

"Oh Felix, where am I? I've had the most awful nightmare."

"Penzi, you're safe now. That's all that matters. Can you lace your arms around my neck so I can pull you out of there? I'm not wearing my opposable thumbs."

She gave a little laugh. *That's my girl.*

I hauled her out. She sank to the floor, her face blanched. A nasty red welt stood out dark against her redhead's pale skin at the side of her collarbone where the taser had struck. She rubbed the patch and peered at it with a frown.

"What happened to me?"

"You were tasered by the witchdoctor, boss. It's been a close run thing. Without the help of the High Council of the Guild of White Witches, I could have lost you."

"The High Council?"

I jerked my head towards the ceiling where the seven witches hovered. The secretary fussed with her papers and whispered, "We should be leaving, your Ladyship. We have many other calls to attend to tonight."

"All in good time," the chief witch answered. "We have to see Mpenzi safely home."

Penzi meanwhile was staring around her. "Where's the witchdoctor?"

I pointed to the pile of ash that had slid off onto the floor when I pushed the coffin lid aside. "Courtesy of the High Council, boss."

Penzi shuddered. "Help me to my feet, Felix."

I pulled Penzi up from the floor and helped her to bang the dust and bits of old bone off from her clothes.

She bowed low before tipping her head up and making eye contact with the chief witch. "Your Ladyship, how can I ever thank you for what you and your council did for me tonight? I don't know the details yet, but Felix tells me your intervention was crucial."

The chief witch nodded. "That's all right, child. The evil witchdoctor of the Wazini has been in our sights for a long time as you know. It was only a matter of time before we had to neutralize him."

Penzi looked at the pile of ash and up at me, whispering, "Neutralize?" under her breath.

"I heard that, Mpenzi," said the chief witch. "We had to finish him off for once and for all. We, too, have discovered he's been living in the tunnels under your house. My heart was in my mouth when we heard he was developing a powder of crushed human bone to attack your protective aura. We couldn't afford to have him kill one of our most promising young white witches. I'm only sorry we were late arriving tonight, but it's been a busy one. Calls from Alaska. Calls from Australia."

Penzi was wilting before my eyes. She needed to get home, have a square meal and a strong drink.

"Your Ladyship," I broke in, "we're stranded. The car is at the dolmen. I must get Penzi home."

"I'm well aware of that, young man. If you go out into the fresh air, she can climb on your back and we'll see to the rest. And please, make sure she sees a doctor tomorrow."

We both bowed. I took Penzi's arm and helped her up the steps out of the vault. I lay down on the ground to allow Penzi to climb on my back. Zuzu came over to us to say goodbye, and we thanked him for his help.

"That's all right," he said. "It'll be *La Toussaint* in a few hours' time. All the families will come to put flowers on the graves, and the children will make a big fuss of me. It's one of the best days of the year for me."

Almost before he'd finished speaking, Penzi and I were sucked into the same flashing bright tunnel of light. Before we had time to realize we were in the tunnel, we were being gently deposited in our kitchen back at *Les Dragons*.

Zig and Zag, our German shepherds woke up, as did our two new kittens. All four of them came bustling around us with much wagging of tails from the dogs and purring from the cats.

"Thank goodness, you're back safely," said Zag. "We couldn't help overhearing your conversation with Gwinny, but there was little we could do. We've been so worried."

Penzi waved them back saying, "Give Felix the space to shift back into his human form."

As I morphed from big cat to faithful bodyguard, Penzi put the kettle on for a hot toddy. We scrounged about for something to eat but couldn't find any biscuits. We had to settle for hot buttered toast with honey from our hives.

And so to bed.

12

When Felix brought me my morning tea in bed on the morning of All Saints' Day, he found me standing by the window looking out over the Atlantic Ocean, trying to make sense of what had happened on Halloween. My memory was sketchy. I'd remember something then it would fly away again out of my reach.

I took the proffered mug of tea and sat back down on my bed. I patted the space beside me, "Come sit with me and tell me all about Halloween."

For the next half an hour he told me the most unbelievable story about the witchdoctor, a giant python, and traveling through space in a bright shining tunnel. If it wasn't for the large scorch mark below my collarbone I would have thought he was pulling my leg. However, as his story unfolded, my memory gradually returned: the pain, the terror, the fear that I'd suffocate in that stone coffin, that something would happen to Felix and no one would know I was trapped in there... that the witchdoctor would win the battle.

When he ended his tale, we sat together in silence, each

feeling thankful everything had turned out all right in the end. Well, almost everything.

"We survived, Felix, and the witchdoctor is dead, reduced to ash, but not everyone has got off lightly in this story. Dubois will have a cold case on his record for ever. He cannot solve a case where the murderer was a supernatural. The mayor may live to fight another term. People's memories are short. But what about Father Pedro and his congregation?"

"I phoned him this morning, boss. He was on his way to the cemetery to bless the vault in which the murder occurred. He wanted to get the blessing of the way before he conducted mass for *La Toussaint*. Apparently, the story about the body had got out and the family in question had asked him to do what he could to set the souls of their ancestors at rest after such a sacrilegious invasion. Fortunately, they don't know some of their ancestors' bones are missing. Father Pedro says what they don't know can't upset them. And he's right, I guess."

"We'll have to make it up to Dubois in the future."

"*Absolument*," Felix said with a grin.

"Did you ask him what happened about the stolen name plaques and the flower vases?"

"Yes. Pierre Lamy found them in a bin bag behind the wall of the cemetery. He managed to stick all the plaques back in time. However, they don't know who the thief was."

"It could have been the vagrant hoping to sell them to make some money to live on."

"If that's why he was in the cemetery, it was an expensive plan. It cost him his life, boss."

"I can't help feeling sorry for him, thief or no thief. He didn't deserve to end up dead in a graveyard after risking all to find a new life."

LATER THAT DAY we made a sortie into the countryside en famille and passed the cemetery. I'd been planning to call in and see if everything was in order, but such a visit proved impossible. Cars were parked all along the verge for miles in every direction. I slowed right down. The cemetery was thronged with celebrants taking flowers to the graves, tombs and vaults of their ancestors. All along the road we overtook people carrying pots of chrysanthemums. Life had returned to normal in our little seaside town of Beaucoup-sur-Mer.

THE DOCTOR, though puzzled by the taser burn, gave me a clean bill of health and some salve to rub on the wound which soon healed. Dubois called me several times during the following weeks, asking for help with the case of the vagrant found in the cemetery. Felix and I went through the motions, but, of course, we couldn't tell him what had really happened when the natural and supernatural worlds had collided. But we would help him in the future, although I hoped it would never be necessary. With my knowledge of the malignant power of evil, I should have known better.

THE END OF BOOK SEVEN
French Country Murders

Now, you may wish to read the first chapter of the next book in this series,
The Witch who Risked the Shot.

THE WITCH WHO RISKED THE SHOT

CHAPTER ONE

What on earth was that dreadful racket?

The dogs were barking their heads off downstairs. I scrambled out of bed and threw on my dressing gown. A loud irregular thumping met me as I flung open my bedroom door and hurried down to find out if the sky was falling in. Zig and Zag, our two German shepherds, snatched themselves away from their defense of our home long enough to flash me a doggy warning look before turning back to their assault on our front door. They wanted out... and now. Zag launched himself at the door again while poor Zig, her belly heavy with puppies, snuffled and snorted at the crack below the door.

I couldn't get to the door to open it. They wouldn't give way. I turned aside and entered the kitchen. Jimbo, my younger brother, and Gwinny, my mother, were leaning out of the front window facing the seawall lining the bay, Jimbo almost falling out, my mother hanging on to his t-shirt at the back.

As I crossed over to join them, possibilities for the excited disturbance ran through my mind: a fight, a delivery van, a helicopter on the beach? Any giveaway aural clues had been overlaid by the dogs' frenzied barking.

Gwinny pointed with her free hand. "Look, Penzi."

Jimbo twisted round when he heard her. "Don't let the dogs out, Penzi. It's too dangerous for them."

Too dangerous for two German shepherds? This I had to see.

I peered over Jimbo's shoulder.

There, on the far side of the road, strutting along the seawall on his businesslike trotters was the most enormous wild boar. The largest I'd ever seen. He had to be at least four feet high and six feet long... at a guess. Whiskers bristling, long snout sniffing the air, he tossed his head from side to side brandishing his deadly curling tusks.

He was heading for the Esplanade. All lethal 300 pounds of him.

Left alone and in their own environment, wild boar are not to be feared. But, riled up and in town, he was as dangerous as an escaped circus lion. His piggy little eyes could make him take offense where none was meant. His weight could turn his tusks into deadly missiles. Set at the right height, those tusks could slice through a man's femoral artery, leaving him to die from loss of blood.

Thank goodness, Jimbo had had the sense not to let the dogs out. They'd have been gored and shredded.

I had to do something about it, but I'd left my phone upstairs.

"Quick, Gwinny, call the Fire Brigade," I said, taking over her hold on Jimbo's shirt.

She snatched her phone from the kitchen table and speed dialed the *pompiers* - the French fire brigade - who are trained to deal with all unexpected emergencies.

The little white poodle from two doors down ran out into the road yapping a challenge at our strange tourist. The boar stopped, shook his head, peered myopically at the dog. His muscles tensed in launch readiness. He was going to wipe that pesky little pup off the face of the earth.

Riding to the rescue like a medieval knight on a charger, came Martine, our postwoman, in her yellow van. She swerved around the dog, flung on the brakes forming a protective barrier against the boar's anticipated charge. And charge he did, straight for Martine's front door, ramming it with his bony head and sideswiping a long scratch all the way along the vehicle as he met an immovable object larger than him.

He shook his head, whether in disbelief or defeat I couldn't guess. Martine opened the window and screamed at the animal to go away. Her language was a little more fruity than that, but the boar got her meaning and moved off on his promenade towards the Esplanade even if not quite so jauntily.

"We have to call the mayor," I said to Gwinny. "That beast could hurt someone, maybe even kill a child."

"On it," she replied, handing the phone to me.

My relationship with Monsieur Bonhomie, the mayor of our little French seaside town of Beaucoup-sur-Mer, has been rocky at times, mostly when he thought that I and my associate, Felix, had not respected the dignity of his office. However, we now worked well together. Felix and I had solved several murders in our little town. Monsieur Bonhomie was grateful for the work we'd done in restoring the faith of visitors in the safety of our town as a vacation destination. Tourism is our town's main earner now that the fishing industry has declined.

He was surprised to hear that a wild boar was parading around the town and as alarmed as I was at the possible danger to the citizens. He said he would call out the gendarmes to help the *pompiers*.

As I swiped off the phone, Gwinny passed me a mug of hot tea. I'm useless in the morning until I've had my dose of an Englishman's panacea of all evil.

Jimbo dropped back into the room. "He's out of sight. I want to follow him and see what happens," he said making for the door.

Gwinny grabbed hold of him before I could.

"No, you don't, young man. That creature could turn and attack you. We'll wait here quietly for the authorities to catch him and take him back to the forest."

Jimbo let out an exasperated sigh but obeyed his grandmother.

I went out into the hall where the dogs had fallen quiet as the perceived danger to their pack had moved on. They lay on the tiled floor, cooling off with their tongues hanging out.

I rubbed their fur with my bare foot as I drank my hot tea. In between sips I told them how silly they were to get so worked up about an animal that couldn't get into the house.

"It's not good for Zig in her condition to become so over-excited," I added.

Zag sat up at that, raised his head and gave me a stare. "Don't you think I know that, Penzi. She's my sister after all. But it's my job to defend this family, especially when Felix isn't around."

That's a point. Where was Felix? How had he missed out on all the kerfuffle?

The slap of his flip-flops preceded his descent of our old oaken stairs.

Rubbing his eyes in his usual pre-coffee daze, he asked, "What the hell's going on down here? Can't a chap have a moment's peace in this house?"

Zag ran to greet him, tail wagging, glad that he could pass the responsibility of defending the family back to Felix who was better equipped to tackle a wild boar than he was.

Felix is my associate, my invaluable sidekick in keeping Beaucoup-sur-Mer and its surroundings free from the evil doings of sundry murderers. He's gorgeous to look at with peridot colored eyes and tawny blond hair. Looks which hint at his alter ego for Felix is a shape shifter, sometimes a leopard, sometimes a Savannah cat. He arrived in the guise of a cat, unannounced as a posthumous gift from my father, Sir Archibald Munro, the famous anthropologist. Felix's remit in life is to protect me from all things evil in the natural world. Although a supernatural himself, he cannot extend this protection to things supernatural. We both need the help of magic for that. I am, of course, a white witch. I haven't always known that, but am now resigned to my destiny as a champion of good against evil. I'm even beginning to like my occupation. Tracking down killers is mentally challenging, and the pay-off when we get our man is so rewarding, an endorphin feast.

"So?" Felix asked again, sitting down on the bottom step and looking at the three of us with bleary eyes.

I quickly explained what was happening.

Felix sprang to his feet. "I'll sort him out," he said.

Oh no. The tips of his ears were turning yellow. He was shifting involuntarily. He couldn't let the townspeople see him as a leopard. Not only would it give away his precious secret second identity, but the sight of a leopard would be far more terrifying than a familiar old boar, dangerous as the porker might be.

I crossed the hall and reaching up, took hold of Felix's ears and gave them a tug.

"Calm down, Felix. You cannot shift now in broad daylight, in front of our fellow citizens. You may catch the wild boar, but you'll scare everyone to death."

He put his hands over mine. A look of astonishment crossed his face as he touched the fur.

"Wow! That's never happened before. I've always had to will the change. What should I do?"

"I don't know. Try some deep breaths while I rub your ears. You probably need to relax."

He breathed in deeply and let his breath out slowly. As I rubbed, the fur disappeared until there was only skin beneath my fingers.

"You're all right now," I said giving him a comradely slap on the shoulder.

He scrambled to his feet and rushed into the kitchen to look out of the window.

"Where's that creature?" he asked.

Jimbo pointed out the gray-brown blob disappearing into the distance in the direction of the Esplanade. From time to time, the boar stopped and snuffled about the cobbles. If he was looking for truffles, he was out of luck.

Felix hurried out of the kitchen calling out, "Pour me some coffee, Gwinny. I'll throw some clothes on. Penzi and I'll follow the creature."

"At a safe distance, I hope," Gwinny interrupted. "And you're not to take Jimbo."

"Oh, no," Jimbo answered, slumping down into a chair in a sulk. "I always miss the fun."

~

When a still disheveled but operational Felix returned, I snatched up my camera. Gwinny handed him a mug of coffee and we made for the front door. And the worst happened. Felix was so busy trying to get out of the door without spilling his coffee that the dogs shot through his legs and ran off down the road after their vanishing quarry.

We followed as quickly as we could, Felix spilling half his coffee down his t-shirt. The boar reached the Esplanade well ahead of us. What a scene and what a noise.

Two fire engines blocked the main entrances to the Esplanade while a couple of blue police vans, sirens blaring and lights flashing, stood across the small lanes running down towards the sea front. From one of the vans a public service announcement blared out a warning to everyone to stay indoors.

Customers peered out from the safety of shop doors and windows. I glanced down at the beach. A gendarme was herding sun worshipers and their children towards a large rock at the end of the beach. Another gendarme was pushing people up onto the rock out of the way of a possible incursion by the wild boar.

The firemen were attempting to trap the creature with crowd control barriers. The boar had other ideas. He rammed the railings repeatedly, stamped and snorted as his tusks rang against the hollow metal. Zig and Zag darted back and forth outside the barriers, barking defiance at the boar.

The mayor called out to me, "Over here, Penzi."

He had managed to get his portly body up onto the top of the Esplanade wall, a safe vantage point.

I shook my head and pointed at my dogs. I had to get

them away from the makeshift enclosure before they got themselves into trouble. I was only a few feet away from them with Felix following me when one of the firemen misjudged the barriers. Before anyone could stop them, Zig and Zag pushed through into the makeshift pen and confronted the boar. Zag took him on from the front while Zig snapped at his rear flank. The boar tossed his head in fury. He sideswiped Zig with his rear haunches, flinging her across the paving stones to crash against the shaky barrier. If Zag hadn't kept the boar's attention on him by darting in and out snapping at the boar's snout, Zig would have been finished. I wasn't sure that she wasn't. I rushed around to the outside of the barrier where she was lying. I put my hand through the bars and felt for a breath or the beat of her heart.

There was no sign of life. I'm ashamed to say I burst into tears. Tough old me. Bulwark of the Munro family. Felix crouched down beside me and enveloped me in his arms. Meanwhile Zag continued to bait the boar and withdraw, advance and retreat, living up to his name. Such a brave dog.

The furor ebbed and flowed until all became silent. No one moved. The boar and Zag froze like a twinned marble sculpture. Reality receded. Time hung.

I came to when Felix shook me and pulled me to my feet.

"Penzi, come on, boss. The vet's here. She's been called in to dart the boar. Brave as they are, the gendarmes and the firemen are unwilling to confront the beast without protective hunting gear."

Dr Julie Bécard reached past me to squat beside Zig. She checked the poor bitch with her stethoscope.

"She's alive. She's breathing. She's in shock. I'll treat her as soon as I've dealt with that tusker. We don't want him to kill your other dog, do we? Meanwhile, you must breathe, too."

I sat back on the cold paving stone and did as I was told. The vet stood over me, her blowpipe swaying from side to side above my head as she tried to find a clean shot to tranquilize the boar without hitting Zag. Meanwhile, our courageous dog, not knowing what was going on, kept veering into target range. How I wanted to call out to him, but I cannot talk to the dogs when there are natural humans about.

Zut! A dart flew out hitting the boar squarely in the left shoulder. The huge creature swayed on his feet and fell over, out cold. All those there, let out a community sigh of relief. Some clapped. Some called out *bravo*. The vet entered the enclosure with her bag, checked the boar and said it was all right to move him. Not an easy task, but not one I stayed to see. Julie moved across to attend to Zig.

She checked Zig's heart and lungs again and nodded with satisfaction. Taking her time, she felt all over for broken bones. She palpated Zig's bellyful of puppies.

"Well?" I asked, anxious to know the worst.

Julie smiled.

"Everything seems all right. We'll give it twenty-four hours. If she shows any signs of distress, we'll have to scan her. Meanwhile, you can take her home and keep her quiet."

"I'll carry her," said Felix, stooping to gather our precious dog in his arms. "Boss, you take Zag."

We thanked Julie and hurried away, leaving the firemen and the gendarmes to the task of hauling the heavy boar onto a trailer for his journey back to the forest.

All in all, the whole town was lucky to have escaped

what could have been a sad ending to the boar's adventure. The boar had injured no one but Zig and both had lived to tell the tale.

~

I hope you enjoyed this first chapter of
The Witch who Risked the Shot.
You will find this book available for sale at your favorite bookseller. Links on my website - katiepenryn.com

~

NOTE FROM KATIE PENRYN

THE PIXIE DUST EFFECT

If you enjoyed this book, I'd love it if you'd pass your enjoyment on to others by leaving a review. Reviews are like pixie dust. Pure magic! They help other readers decide whether to read my books, and they pump me full of endorphins, firing up my imagination and making me thump away at the old keyboard with renewed enthusiasm to get my stories out faster.

Join my Readers' Group on my website and receive a free coloring book suitable for all ages, KatiePenryn.com, or on my Facebook page, Facebook.com/KatiePenryn.Author

French Country Murders

Book 1: The Witch who Couldn't Spell
Book 2: The Witch who Loved Eclairs

Book 3: The Witch who Got the Blues
Book 4: The Witch who Found a Pearl
Book 5: The Witch who Saved Christmas
Book 6: The Witch who Foiled the Plot
Book 7: The Witch who Hated Halloween
Book 8: The Witch who Risked the Shot
Book 9: The Witch who Picked a Poppy
Book 10: The Witch who Forged a Monet
- Jan 2022
Book 11: The Witch who Tipped the Scales
- Mar 2022

This series is also available in Large Print and Ebook.

Our Man in Mazita

Book 1: Beau—ootiful Soo—oop!
Book 2 : Something Spotted
Book 3: Something Rotten
Book 4: Christmas in Mazita

To view these and my other books, please visit my website, KatiePenryn.com, or my Author Page on your favorite bookseller's site.

You can write to me at katiepenryn@gmail.com. I love hearing from you. Knowing that there's someone out there who has brought my book to life through their own imagination is a wonderful feeling. I answer all emails and Facebook messages personally.

30.xi.21

GLOSSARY

French words and expressions:

absolument – absolutely

mes amis – my friends

amour propre – lit. self-love, used in English, self-respect

la bavette – a thin cheaper steak, skirt

bonne idée – that's a good idea

bonsoir – good evening

BB – Brigitte Bardot, a beloved and sexy French filmstar of the '50s and '60s

une brocante – something between an antiques shop and a bric-à-brac shop

une casse-croûte – a snack, literally "break-crust", meaning a piece broken off a loaf of bread

ça suffit! – that's enough!

le cafard – lit. cockroach, the French for the blues (misery not music!)

le cantonnier – the gardener, general handyman of a village – from the word "canton" – several communes make up one canton.

Combien? – how much?

une commune – is a level of administrative division in the French Republic. French communes are analogous to civil townships and incorporated municipalities in the United States. The United Kingdom has no exact equivalent, as communes resemble districts in urban areas, but are closer to parishes in rural areas where districts are much larger. Communes are based on historical geographic communities or villages and have received significant powers of governance to manage the populations and land of the geographic area covered. The communes are the fourth-level administrative divisions of France. Each commune has a mayor.

"Dames" – ladies' cloakroom/bathroom

déjà-vu – used in English, means "already seen"

un demi – lit. a half, used for drinks especially beer/lager meaning half a liter

deux-chevaux – lit. two-horses, a little French car Citroën with two h.p.

les dragons – the dragons

faisant les cents pas – lit. doing a hundred steps, pacing up and down

en famille – used in English; to do something as a family, together

et alors? – what next ? So ?

épuisé(e) - exhausted

la farine – flour

un gendarme – see item below, a policeman who has a military background

la gendarmerie – the station were the gendarmes hang out, roughly speaking like a police station, but the gendarmes are not policemen as such. The Gendarmerie Nationale is part of the French armed forces. It has the primary responsibility for policing smaller towns and rural areas, as well as the armed forces and military installations, airport security and shipping ports. Being a military force, the gendarmerie has a highly centralized organization structure. It is under the control of both the Ministry of Defense and the Ministry of the Interior (as far as its civil duties are concerned).

faux-filet – lit. a false fillet steak, a sirloin steak

un gâteau – a cake

kir royale – a French cocktail, a variation on Kir. It consists of crème de cassis topped with champagne

le livret de famille – family record kept by the mayor's office

une madeleine– a buttery little sponge cake usually shaped like a scallop shell

le maire – the mayor, the administrator of a commune. He is voted for by the rate-paying residents, including non-citizens.

la mairie – the mayor's office; in a large town or city, this would be the Town Hall.

mais oui – but yes, of course

Maître – lit. master, used to France as an honorary title for a lawyer/advocate

malheuresement – unfortunately

Le Marché de Sables – Market of the Sands

la maternelle – nursery school

le méchoui – a spit roasted pig or sheep (from the Arabic)

le métier – profession, occupation

merci mille fois – thank-you a thousand times

le merguez – long thin highly spiced sausage

naturellement! – naturally!

des objets-d'art – used in English; small pieces of art such as sculptures, enameled jewellery boxes

Le Palais des Blues – the Blues Palace

une pâtisserie – a cake shop and/or a pastry

ma/mon pauvre petit(e) – my poor little one
pineau – is an aperitif from the Charente/Dordogne departments. It is a fortified wine of the same strength as sherry and comes in a red or a white version. Often served over ice.
Punaise! – lit. a shield-shaped green bug that stinks when touched. Used as a mild swear word
Salut! – Hi ! Informal
Sympa – an adjective meaning companionable, friendly, an okay person
thé à l'anglais – tea English style with milk
La Toussaint – All Saints' Day
tout de suite – at once, immediately
trop dégueulasse! – too disgusting!
Vade mecum – the Latin for "come with me"; often used for an indispensable item such as a diary, travel guide

Other references:

Banksy- is an anonymous England-based street artist. His satirical street art and subversive epigrams combine dark humor with graffiti executed in a distinctive stenciling technique.
dolmen – is a prehistoric arrangement of large stone blocks, with one horizontally straddling two uprights to make an arch. Their origin and use are uncertain, but they were probably the entrance to tombs which have since disappeared.
Laphroaig – the golden single malt scotch whisky from the Isle of Islay in the Hebrides, famous for its distinctive peaty flavor
Leopardmen – these men are part of African folklore
Send someone to Coventry –an English expression meaning

to stop speaking to someone, i.e. stop social contact with them

Sowhat – is an anonymous Parisian street artist

Venn diagram – A diagram using overlapping circles to show areas of correspondence